A MOST DANGEROUS WEAKNESS

Crispin's eyes blazed as he told Phillipa, "You threaten to end our betrothal. But make no mistake, you shall be my wife."

Phillipa forced up her chin to meet his eyes squarely. "I would rather spend the rest of my life walled into a convent than marry you."

A faint smile that held no mirth curved his lips. "Really? Yet when I held you in my arms, I fancy you felt something quite different." Color suffused her cheeks and he laughed. "My dear, what a very poor libertine I should be if I were not sensitive to the smallest response in my prey."

"It is your conceit that imagined it," she said fiercely.

"Do you think it might be that?" he asked, and before she could turn her head away, he caught and held her face in an iron grip so that she could not evade his lips —or choke off the infamous feeling flooding her. . . .

THE WORTH INHERITANCE

[For a list of other Signet Regency Romances by Elizabeth Hewitt, please turn the page. . . .]

The Worth Inheritance

Elizabeth Hewitt

A SIGNET BOOK

NEW AMERICAN LIBRARY

PUBLISHED BY
THE NEW AMERICAN LIBRARY
OF CANADA LIMITED

NAL BOOKS ARE AVAILABLE AT QUANITY DISCOUNTS WHEN USED TO
PROMOTE PRODUCTS OR SERVICES. FOR INFORMATION PLEASE WRITE
TO PREMIUM MARKETING DIVISION, NEW AMERICAN LIBRARY,
1633 BROADWAY, NEW YORK, NEW YORK 10019

First Printing, July, 1986

2 3 4 5 6 7 8 9

SIGNET TRADEMARK REG. U.S. PAT. OFF. AND FOREIGN COUNTRIES
REGISTERED TRADEMARK—MARCA REGISTRADA
HECHO EN WINNIPEG, CANADA

SIGNET, SIGNET CLASSIC, MENTOR, PLUME, MERIDIAN
AND NAL BOOKS are published in Canada by The New American
Library of Canada, Limited, 81 Mack Avenue, Scarborough,
Ontario, Canada M1L 1M8

PRINTED IN CANADA
COVER PRINTED IN U.S.A.

1

Philippa Worth made an errant stitch in the lace she was attaching to a silk underdress and with some difficulty suppressed an unladylike oath. If she had been alone, she might have voiced the expletive, but a slight young man, very like her in features but fair where she was dark, paced back and forth in front of the tall windows overlooking the rear garden. In truth, it was owing to his presence and obvious impatience that Philippa was deprived of her usual skill with the needle. She was about to adjure him to find some other occupation, or at least another location, when she was forestalled by the entrance of her aunt's butler, Johnson.

Sir Aubery Worth ceased his pacing at once and turned abruptly toward the door, his expression hopeful. But the servant paid him not the least heed, bowing instead before Philippa and proffering a silver tray on which reposed a folded cream-colored piece of paper.

Before Philippa could put down her needle and take the paper, Aubery sped across the room and snatched it from the tray. "Blast! Damn and blast," he exploded, and threw the paper down on the tray still

5

held by the startled butler. Aubery returned to the windows to stare out at the garden in a disconsolate way.

Philippa knew better than to apologize for Aubery's impulsive behavior before a servant, but the temptation to do so was strong, for she liked Lady Carnavon's principal servant and she was completely out of charity with her brother. But she simply thanked Johnson with what dignity she could muster, and took the paper. She glanced at it quickly and saw that it was only a note from her aunt reminding her to have her maid press her costume for the masquerade ball they were to attend at Lady MacReath's that evening.

Philippa had guessed the contents of the note from its appearance, but for reasons of her own, she was as anxious for the arrival of the post, as was her brother, and was disappointed that the butler had nothing more for her. Hasn't the post arrived yet, Johnson?" she asked the butler before dismissing him.

"Yes, Miss Worth," he replied. "The post arrived this half-hour since, but it was most meager today. There were several of the usual invitations addressed to her ladyship, but other than that the only letters were for his lordship and Miss Carteret."

Philippa could not quite keep her face from falling, and seeing what appeared to be curiosity creep into the kindly servant's expression, she said quickly to deflect interest away from herself, "Sir Aubery is expecting a letter from our cousin Lord Tamary that he is most anxious to receive. If anything arrives for him from Scotland, whether by post or by hand, please let us know at once."

"Of course, miss," said Johnson, and permitted himself the ghost of a smile. Everyone in the Carnavon household was cognizant of the fact that Sir Aubery was currently besotted of a young lady of great beauty and little fortune, but this romance was not taken very seriously belowstairs, for, as the saying went, the young baronet was "in the petticoat line." It was also known that Sir Aubery had written to his cousin who was also his guardian for permission to honorably pay his addresses to his beloved. But it was not the first time Sir Aubery had written a similar letter, and it was assumed by one and all that Dominic Worth, ninth Baron Tamary, a man whose views on youthful marriage and an excess of romanticism were not sympathetic, would reply as he had before: that his ward should wait until he had reached his majority and the control of his own affairs before embarking on a major commitment to any young woman.

And yet here was Miss Worth, seeming as concerned as her brother what the answer should be; perhaps there was more to Sir Aubery's latest fancy than mere calf love. Johnson's interest was piqued to the point that he ventured a bit more information to see if it would garner him the like. "There *was* a letter from Scotland today, miss, for his lordship. It wasn't franked by Lord Tamary, though."

But the servant's seed did not bear fruit. Philippa merely nodded in an absent way. "I expect it was from the solicitor with whom he has been dealing concerning the sale of some property near Edinburgh," she said, and then thanked the butler in a way that was clearly dismissive.

"Damn him," Aubery said. "It's just like Cousin Dominic to keep me cooling my heels waiting for an answer when he must know my whole future depends on it. It is absurd that I should have a blasted guardian, at my age!"

Philippa did not point out to Aubery that he was still six months shy of one-and-twenty and could not legally manage his own affairs even without the restrictions of their father's will. This document, much disliked and endlessly discussed between the Worths, continued the guardianship, at least of all financial matters, until Aubery reached the age of five-and-twenty if he married and thirty if he did not.

Philippa put aside her work and went over to the windows. "You know that Cousin Dominic is an indifferent correspondent," she said, linking an arm in his. "And since he had that attack of apoplexy last fall, he has been a near invalid. Perhaps he hasn't been well enough to answer you himself and doesn't like to entrust the writing of such a delicate matter to another."

"If the answer were yes, there would be nothing delicate about it," Aubery said gloomily. "Just because he never married himself he has this notion that one should be quite ancient before even thinking of getting leg-shackled. I'll wager he never read the half of what I wrote to him explaining how *I* felt and how wonderful Lydia is."

"Well, it was a rather lengthy letter," Philippa said lightly, hoping to tease him out of his dark humor. "Perhaps it has taken him this long to finish it."

But Aubery shrugged off her lightness and her arm, crossing the room to resume his agitated pacing. "The worst of it is that I have given Lydia the hint of my intentions but I cannot speak when I haven't the right to manage my own affairs. And Hobarth has been dangling after her this past month; he means to offer for her, I am certain of it. He'll cut me out and there won't be a damned thing I can do about it."

"If her heart is so easily captured," Philippa said dampeningly, "then perhaps you should let Hobarth have it." She privately thought that Miss Lydia Wright was a very lovely girl who unfortunately had more hair than wit, and who, once her girlish loveliness had faded, would heartily bore the mercurial Sir Aubery.

"You don't understand. She is an angel, an innocent. She cares nothing for the world, but her mother is a veritable dragon. Lady Wright is determined to get the best match she can for Lydia, and if Hobarth hasn't my fortune, he is heir to a barony and what he has is respectable enough and his to settle as he pleases, whereas I am at the mercy of others for my pin money. If only Cousin Dominic weren't so dashed stubborn."

Like all of the Worths, Philippa thought. Their father, Sir Matthew Worth, had had views not unlike those of his brother concerning the responsibility of youth, and he had carried these to the point of so tying up his considerable fortune after his death that his children lived as near pensioners on their own estate. It was not that their allowances were inadequate, but every penny spent had to be justified and any extra expenses approved by a trio of appointed guardians set up by Sir Matthew's will. One of these guardians, Sir Walter Carteret, had died within a year of Sir Matthew, but even with only two guardians, all financial requests and other permissions required time and some difficulty to be acted upon. For a goodly portion of the year Aubery and Philippa lived at Maverly Hall with one of their guardians, Lord Maverly, but Lord Maverly, not being a Worth himself and so inclined to occasional uncertainty, usually expressed his views dependent on those of Lord Tamary, who, as Aubery frequently declared, was opinionated enough for two.

Philippa, who was possessed of a determined chin and a mouth that could be willful, readily admitted that she, too, could be obstinate, though she preferred to think of it as determination rather than inflexibility. Her future, too, was restricted by the terms of her father's will, though in a different way. When she had attained her majority the previous year, she ceased to be in the control of her guardians except for the pin-money allowance that she received from the estate. But though the amount set aside for her dowry could now be bestowed freely on whomever she herself might choose for a husband, the amount was ludicrously small for a young woman whose family was known to have wealth. Sir Matthew, whose reasoning it was that an unprotected heiress might easily fall prey to a clever fortune-hunter, had seen to it that this could not happen to his daughter. There *was* a stipulation in Sir Matthew's will suggesting that Aubery, if he deemed it prudent, could increase Philippa's portion after Aubery himself came into the estate, but it was an entirely voluntary matter and of no value at all on the marriage market, particularly as it might be a fair number of years before Sir Aubery could honor that hope and as he was, in any case, under no obligation to do so.

"I think," she said cautiously, but still with a flat inflection, "that if Miss Wright is, ah, right for you, she will refuse Hobarth whatever her mama's urgings. I should never marry anyone but the man of my choosing no matter what difficulties might be cast in my way."

"But Lydia is nothing like you," Aubery said in a way that sounded suspiciously critical. "She is a sweet child, the most dutiful of daughters."

"Biddable" was the word that came to Philippa, and it was as well for the peace between brother and sister that the word remained unsaid. At the moment the door opened and Miss Lianna Carteret, daughter of the deceased guardian and cousin to Aubery and Philippa, came into the room. Lianna wore a dressing gown tied hastily over an underdress and her raven hair was still unbound. "Pip, I don't know what I am to do," she said woefully. "You *must* help me."

"Of course, if I can," Philippa said readily, glad of any diversion from Aubery's mooncalf sighs.

Aubery, wallowing happily in his own troubles, was not as pleased to be interrupted. "What is it now, widgeon?" he asked quizzingly, but with a faint note of annoyance. "Misplace your hair ribbons?"

"It is no such thing," Lianna said with a pretty pout. She removed a crumpled piece of paper from a pocket in her dressing gown and handed it to Philippa. "I suppose I never should have allowed it to come to this, but I knew there would be a dreadful fuss if I went to Mama, and I would not wish to wound him in any way. It is not his fault if I cannot return his regard."

Philippa barely heard this, as she instantly began to peruse the letter she had been given. She recognized the handwriting at once. Her heart began to beat a little faster and her stomach felt as if she had swallowed lead. It was with admirable composure that she schooled her features to remain impassive as she read:

My lovely,

I can bear it no longer. I must make you mine and tonight shall be our night. You demur, but I know it is only your sweet, modest nature that holds back your heart. Come to me, beloved, don't let the world convince you that you are casting yourself away on a younger son, for I shall do great things with you at my side.

I know you go to Lady MacReath's tonight. At midnight, when everyone is at supper, you must slip away and come to me. All the world (including your mama) believes me in Leicester with friends, so there will be no risk to your fair

name. We may spend an hour in bliss setting out
our future and I shall at last prove to you that we
are a perfect matching. I shall await you in the
lane beside the box garden. You must wear the
violet domino your mama gave you and keep
your mask on even in the garden. These pre-
cautions are necessary, my love, to protect you.
Do not fail me, my only one. It may be weeks
before we dare risk another meeting such as this.

It was not signed, but Philippa knew well enough
who had penned the flowery periods. In her own
bureau, tied together with silk ribbon and carefully
hidden from the prying eyes of servants, were a half-
dozen similar letters. Though none made the bold
request of an hour alone in a dark garden, the style
and sentiments were strikingly similar.

In spite of Philippa's excellent self-command,
Aubery knew her too well to be deceived. He recognized the stricken look that came into her eyes and was
quickly banished, and knew something was amiss. He
twitched the letter out of her fingers and examined it
briefly to extract its general import. His brow instantly
clouded. "Of all the scurvy . . ." he began, but was cut
short by the gentle touch of his sister's hand and the
warning look in her eyes.

"I had not realized that you had formed an attachment for Francis, Lia," Philippa said evenly.

"But I haven't! *He* has formed one for me, and I do
wish he had not!" Lianna spoke with such feeling there
was no doubting her sincerity. "It is not even decent
that he should do so. He is my brother."

"Only in a manner of speaking," Aubery pointed
out. "Your mother married his father long after you
both were born. There's no shared blood between you;
you're not even cousins."

"But when we came here to live, Mama said I must think of Francis and Crispin as my brothers, and I have never thought of either of them in any other way. But isn't there something called a list of kindred that says that you must not marry close relatives by blood or marriage? I couldn't marry Francis if I wished to do so, could I?" she said somewhere between a statement and a question.

"The list of affinity and kindred. But there are such things as dispensations," said Aubery helpfully, and earned a baleful look from his cousin and another fierce glance from his sister.

"Francis seems very sure of you," Philippa said quietly. "It seems surprising that he should be so if you have not encouraged him."

"I have tried to convince him that I do not care for him in that way, but he insists on believing that it is only modesty and the fear that Mama would not approve the match," Lianna said a little petulantly. "He is forever making up to me when I am alone and least expecting it so that I am usually flustered and scarcely know what to say to him."

Aubery exchanged a meaningful glance with his sister, and Philippa looked quickly away. " 'I find you physically displeasing and intellectually tedious' should do the trick," Aubery suggested in a dry way.

"As if I would say such a thing," Lianna said scornfully. "And in any case, I do not feel that way. I like Francis very well, why should I not? It is only that I do not at all wish to marry him. I have tried very hard not to hurt his sensibilities or to make a fuss that would involve Mama, for I think that would be very uncomfortable for us all. Only I suppose it has not been enough if he believed I would meet him tonight in such a way. What should I do, Pip?"

Philippa took the letter from Aubery and returned it to Lianna. "Don't meet him," she said succinctly.

"Suppose he comes into the ball to fetch me?"

"He will hardly do that when he has stressed the need for discretion and the fact that he will not be expected," Philippa replied.

"But if he is masked, he may come into the house without being recognized," Lianna insisted. "And even if he does not, he will probably try to coerce me into another meeting at some other time."

"Then you must become stronger in your rejection of him and convince him that you mean what you say," Philippa said with what Lianna found to be a strange look of sympathy.

"Oh," said the younger girl, clearly disappointed. "I was sure you would know exactly what I should say or do to put him at a distance for good. You are so much more clever than I."

Philippa gave a short, dry laugh. "Am I?" she said in an enigmatic way. She went back to the table where she had left the underdress and workbasket, and began to put her sewing implements away. She sighed and added in an easier manner, "Well, I shall try to think of something, Lia. But beyond telling you not to meet him in Lady MacReath's garden and to be certain when you see him next to tell him in terms he cannot possibly misunderstand that you cannot return his regard, I don't know that I shall think of anything better."

But this promise was enough to please the younger girl who looked upon Philippa more as an older sister than a cousin and who had regarded Philippa as her confident and adviser since earliest childhood days. Lianna cast her arms about Philippa and hugged her. "I knew you would not fail me," she cried. Her objective obtained, she had not the least doubt that Philippa would find the solution to her dilemma. Her usual bright spirits were instantly restored, and exclaiming that she had to go out at once to purchase new ribbons for the shepherdess costume she meant to wear that evening, she flitted out of the room, leaving brother and sister alone again.

After a few moments Aubery began to speak, but Philippa forestalled him. "Please do not say 'I told you so,' Aubery," she begged. "I am well aware that my judgment has been at fault without the added insult of having it pointed out to me." She dropped the scissors she held in her hand and sank abruptly into the chair next to the table, burying her face in her hands.

Aubery, his own problems forgotten for the moment, went at once to her side. "Don't cry, love," he said, laying a comforting hand on her shoulder. "Francis Glennon isn't worth your tears."

"I am not crying," Philippa said, and raised her head to show that she was dry-eyed. "I am trying to understand what has happened. Did you know that Francis had an interest in Lia?"

"No, of course not," Aubery assured her. "He damn well would have heard from me if I had. Leave it to Lia to come to you with this. Only a ninny like her would fail to realize what's plain as a pikestaff to the rest of us: that you've been wearing your heart on your sleeve for Francis Glennon since you were in the schoolroom."

Philippa looked stricken. "Aubery! I have not been that obvious, surely?"

He saw that he had discomfited her and hastened to assure her that it was not that. "I daresay it just seems so to me because I know how you go about sighing for Francis every time we remove from London or Dore-mire." He moved a little away from her, pulling up the straight-backed chair next to hers and sitting straddled across the seat. "I like Francis well enough myself, but he's just an average sort of chap; I never understood what there was in him to attach you so firmly. You've had three Seasons and a respectable court of admirers that you've never encouraged, but there's never been anyone else for you, has there?"

Philippa shook her head sadly. "No. I think I fell in love with him the first day we came to visit Aunt Charlotte after she had remarried to Lord Carnavon. I've always believed that Francis and I would be married one day, whatever obstacles our equal want of fortune might create." Sudden tears stung her eyes, but she brushed them away impatiently. "I *have* been a fool, haven't I?"

"You may safely leave Francis to me," Aubery said in a voice that boded ill for the absent Lord Francis Glennon. "It's damned obvious that he's been trifling with your affections and I don't think he will much like the penalty I have in mind for him."

"I won't have any fuss or scandal about this," Philippa said firmly. "I shall deal with Francis myself."

"There won't be any fuss," Aubery promised. "He shall simply find it to his advantage to rusticate for a time until he is presentable enough for polite society again."

"No," Philippa said, and it was a command. "I will not figure as an object of pity or derision even to myself. If I have been mistaken in my affections for Francis, I shall deal with the consequences of it myself."

"If," Aubery said forcefully. "You can't be *that* besotted. He has been making up to your own cousin under your nose."

"It isn't easy for me to admit, but I suppose I must

see that it is not hard to understand why he would be dazzled by Lia; she is very lovely."

"And a considerable heiress," Aubery said with a sneer.

Philippa averted her eyes from his and put the last of the lace and thread into her workbasket. "Perhaps it is that." She stood and prepared to leave the room. "If you are afraid that I mean to do nothing or easily forgive Francis for allowing me to believe he returned my regard, you need not be. He shall know that I am aware of his perfidy, and he shall pay the price for it as well."

Aubery was not at all sure that he believed her, but with her refusal of his offer of help and his preoccupation with his own troubled romance, he allowed the matter to drop, only adding that if Francis were ever foolish enough to attempt to gain her affections again, he would be very happy to show him his place.

Philippa had one or two chores to see to before she could seek the seclusion of her room without fear of interruption. Unlike Lia, there was no one to whom she could go to seek advice. For the five years that she had been in love with Francis Glennon, she had kept her counsel, sharing her romantic problems and dreams with no one, believing Francis when he told her it was in their best interests to be discreet in their affection for each other.

When her Aunt Charlotte, then Lady Carteret, the relict of Sir Walter Carteret, had married the widowed Marquess of Carnavon, Philippa and Aubery had been invited to spend the Christmas holidays with their aunt at Doremire Abbey, Lord Carnavon's principal seat in Sussex. It would be excessive to say that she had fallen in love with Francis when she had

first met him on her arrival at Doremire, but certainly
she had found herself exceedingly attracted to him,
and when the following spring she had gone to London
to make her curtsy to the world under the auspices of
Lady Carnavon, no other young man who had taken
an interest in her was able to compare to Lord Francis
in her estimation.

Her regard for Francis was strengthened rather than
lessened by the fact that she lived much of the year in
Berkshire with her uncle, Lord Maverly, and only
spent a few months in the spring during the Season and
a month or so at Christmastime in Francis' company.
She did not like to think that she went about sighing
for Francis when they were apart, as Aubery had said,
but Francis was much in her thoughts, and in her own
mind she tended to regard all time she was away from
Francis as time to be bided until they could be together
again.

Ever since the time, about a month after her
presentation, that Francis had admitted, during a
romantic stroll through Vauxhall Gardens, that he felt
for her as she felt for him, she had felt certain of their
future together and regarded with complacency the
time they must wait until they could be wed. She supposed now that she had been too trusting and naive,
but she had seen nothing amiss at Francis' suggestion
that they keep their regard for each other a private
thing. Francis was a younger son of a family known
more for their antiquity than for their fortune, and if
he was to get on in the world, he would have to do so
by means of his own labors.

There were not many options open to the scions of
old families; the church, the military, and politics
were among the few careers deemed respectable by the
aristocracy, and many younger sons sought the "easy"
solution of marrying as well as they could manage.

Merchants and bankers might be sneered at as cits and mushrooms, but their well-dowered daughters were sought after.

Lord Francis Glennon, who was not of a particulary religious turn, nor at all enamored of the romance of soldiering, had opted for a political career, and Philippa thought it was all to his credit that he should love her, a relatively portionless woman, instead of joining the ranks of fortune-hunters. And when Francis told her that the world would not understand their finer feelings and would condemn them both for chosing love over self-interest, Philippa knew enough of the world to believe him. An impecunious young man with a slowly rising but hopeful political career would be held a fool if he did not marry well, either gaining a fortune or creating a political alliance. So, when he pleaded discretion so that no one might guess they were more to each other than connections by marriage, she agreed, putting his best interests above her own longing for them to be together.

But Philippa in all honesty knew that she was somewhat caught up in the romance of it all. Except for the want of fortune on both sides, there could be no objection to their matching, so the discretion the furtherance of his career required added that bit of spice that might otherwise be lacking. Though they frequently resided under the same roof, it was the stolen moments together, arranged trysts not unlike the one he planned tonight with Lianna, that fed her passion for him.

Philippa was hurt and angry with Francis, but an innate sense of fairness could not entirely blame him for his perfidy. Lianna was beautiful and, as her brother had pointed out, an heiress; perhaps with their own relationship stalled indefinitely, the combination had proved irresistible. Yet Philippa had given her heart to Francis and she truly believed her feelings were reciprocated. In any case, it was not in her nature to abandon five years of devotion at the first bit of trouble. She might hate what Francis was doing, but she could only love him.

Yet neither could she allow his behavior to go unremarked. She wished him to know that she knew of his betrayal and that she was not above wanting him to be punished, at least a little, for the hurt he had done to her. Philippa at once discarded the idea of being cutting to him when next they met, nor did she wish to simply confront him the next time they could be private. She felt this would cast her in the image of a pitiable, scorned, and rejected woman, and this filled her with repugnance.

But Philippa's mind was facile, and by the time Susan, the maid she shared with Lianna when visiting her aunt, arrived to help her dress for dinner and the ball, she had formed a clever plan that would not only deliver to Francis a proper come-uppance and make it clear to him she was not to be trifled with, but that had about it the air of an adventure which was not without risk. It in every way appealed to her.

2

The dowager Marchioness of Carnavon sighed with resignation. She supposed that since they were already under way on their journey to Lady MacReath's masquerade ball, there was no point in continuing the argument she and her niece had been having since dinner, for the point was moot. For no good reason that she could fathom, Philippa had insisted that she did not wish to wear the costume she had had made for the ball and instead was wearing a simple gray silk evening dress over which she had cast her cousin's violet domino. It had not served in the least to point out to Philippa that the Tudor court dress she had had made might languish in her wardrobe for months before another similar invitation would permit her to wear the costume, and not even the bald statement that violet was a color that made her complexion sallow had answered. Philippa had insisted that the domino was what she wished to wear and had done so over all common sense of protest.

Lianna, usually fairly biddable, had curiously taken her cousin's side—though admitting that violet satin was not truly becoming to Philippa—and she had insisted that if it was what Philippa wished to wear to

21

the ball, she should have it. Aubery, who might have been counted on for a blunt appraisal of his sister's appearance, had already departed for an engagement of his own by the time that Philippa had come down to dinner. Francis, Lady Carnavon believed, was visiting friends in Leicester, and her elder stepson, Crispin, merely commented that he liked the gray silk well enough before he, too, left to take dinner with friends, so the marchioness had found herself without ally. She supposed she was making a lot of the matter, but such capricious behavior was quite out of character for her niece and the dowager could not quite let it go.

"The honey-colored velvet brought out the best in your coloring," Lady Carnavon said into a silence that had grown a little tense in the confines of the carriage.

Lianna, obviously affected by the continuing disagreement, shifted uneasily, but when Philippa spoke, her voice held neither rancor nor weariness. "I know, Aunt Charlotte," she said easily, "but I thought it a bit warm for velvet tonight. Lady Saxe has said she may have a masquerade before we retire from town at the end of the Season, and I shall wear the gown then."

"And doubtless the end of June shall find it cooler than the middle of April," the dowager said tartly, but the carriage had slowed as they approached MacReath House and she at last turned the subject to comment on the facade of the mansion, which was situated a little beyond town near Richmond and stood in ample grounds, a luxury denied to most who had houses within the confines of the city.

Because the ladies traveled without male escort, it was a footman who handed them down from their carriage and who assisted Philippa into her domino. She donned the matching half-mask as they entered the house, but she left the hood of the domino hanging loose behind her. It didn't matter yet that it could be seen that her hair was only brown, not black, and in the dark of the garden Francis would not see that the eyes he peered into were brown instead of blue. Violet, along with black and scarlet, was a common color for dominoes, and Philippa knew there would be many others dressed similarly tonight so that she would be in no way remarkable.

Lady MacReath's ball would unquestionably be described on the following day as a dreadful squeeze. Long before the clocks in the house began to chime the hour of midnight, the ballroom was filled to overflowing and the card rooms and various anterooms were never unoccupied. In spite of the crowd, Philippa recognized a number of her friends, and neither she nor Lianna was allowed to sit out a singal dance until supper.

If Francis had decided to come into the house after all, under cover of a mask, Philippa saw no one she thought might be him. She did recognize Crispin from across the ballroom about an hour after her arrival, for he, like many of the men, wore only a black domino, and though his mask was in place, she could not mistake his tall, erect, athletic figure. But it was unlikely that he would take any greater interest in her appearance now than he had before they had left Carnavon House. She had no fear at all of meeting her brother, who planned to spend the evening with friends at the Daffy Club. Miss Wright would not be attending the masquerade and the entertainment held no other great attraction for Aubery, who thought balls and other mixed social events boring unless brightened by the presence of his latest flirt.

When it had first occurred to Philippa that, disguised by the domino, she might take Lianna's place in the garden to place Francis in the awkward position of making love to the wrong woman, Aubery's planned absence for the evening had made the scheme feasible. Lady Carnavon might not be able to fathom the reason that Philippa had discarded her lovely costume in favor of a plain domino, but Aubery, having read the letter that Francis had sent to Lianna and being familiar with the devious intricacies of his sister's mind, would have known at once what she was about and would certainly have forbidden it, making a fuss if necessary to force her to his will.

As midnight approached, Philippa felt a little natural misgiving about going through with her ruse, but the memory of the endearments that Francis had lavished upon Lianna in his letter strengthened her resolve to serve him out in the manner he deserved. She would not, of course, disclose her identity to him at once; she meant to keep her face lowered in a shy, demure way and trusted to the indistinct light of the moon to make her features inobvious. She intended that Francis should first commit himself and then discover his mistake.

Philippa was engaged for the last dance before supper, but she declined the offer of her partner to take her into supper, claiming that she was already bespoken. This was not true, for she had already refused several similar offers. Philippa did not wish for an escort with whom she would be expected to remain until they returned to the ballroom. She went into supper in the midst of several couples so that her lack of an escort would not be noted. She also thought it prudent that her aunt should see that she had at least come in to supper lest Lady Carnavon find her absence suspicious and remark on it. Philippa spoke briefly with her aunt and several of her friends, but declined all invitations to sit with any of them, claiming, in a vague way, to be promised to someone else.

As soon as she felt she had accomplished her purpose, Philippa left the room as unobtrusively as possible. There were only a few people in the hall, talking in small groups and none of whom Philippa really knew. She started down the stairs to the ground floor as if she intended to visit the ladies' robing room. Fortunately, Lady MacReath was a particular friend of her aunt's and Philippa was well acquainted with the house. At the bottom of the staircase she turned, not right in the direction of the robing room, but left toward the bookroom, which she knew had an entrance into the gardens. Neither the guests nor any servant paid her the least heed.

But as Philippa turned into the hall of the east wing, which led to the bookroom, she heard footsteps hastening toward her and turned to see Lianna behind her, unmasked and a little breathless. "I haven't been able to think of anything but your scheme to trick Francis, Pip, and I can't let you go on with it," Lianna said, catching Philippa by one arm as if to hold her physically from going on.

Conscious that they were still within sight and possible earshot of the numerous servants going about their duties, Philippa put a finger to her lips and led Lianna into the east-wing hall, which was only dimly lit from the light of the main hall at one end and moonlight from a window at the other. "Don't be silly, Lia," Philippa said sharply. "Of course I shall go on with it." She had her own concerns for the success of her scheme, and she did not need to hear objections to it from her one ally.

When Philippa had told Lianna what she meant to do, Lianna had at first thought it a perfect answer to her problem, for Francis would surely believe that she and Philippa were amusing themselves at his expense and his pride would be sufficiently wounded to convince him at last that Lianna was not being demure when she rejected his unwanted advances. But not of an adventurous nature herself, Lianna, with her fertile imagination, had quickly begun to conjure all manner of unpleasantness and danger that might attend Philippa's masquerade. At first Philippa's assurances had dismissed her fears, but as the time for execution of the plan approached, she was again fraught with anxiety.

"I should never have agreed to this; it is a stupid thing to do," she said. "Francis will be furious."

Philippa's lips twitched into a dry smile. "I daresay he won't find our rendezvous in the rose garden romantic at all." Knowing that Lianna, unlike her brother, had not guessed her attachment to Francis, Philippa had decided against confiding in Lianna the truth of her motive in playing this trick on Francis. Once again the image of herself as an object of pity had arisen, and it only strengthened her resolve to bring Francis firmly to heel once and for all. As the outcome of this she did not mean to give Francis his congé; she had already all but forgiven him for allowing himself to be dazzled by Lianna. What she intended was that he be made to realize how nearly he had come to losing her and that if he wished to maintain her affection, he must at last come up to scratch and declare himself openly. Philippa no longer believed in the efficacy of prudence and discretion.

Lianna's brow knit. "You mean in the box garden. The letter said that I was to meet him there."

"No, it was the rose garden," Philippa insisted. "The box garden is very near the house. With the stress Francis has placed on discretion he wouldn't choose a meeting place that might not prove private."

"The rose garden *is* more private and more

romantic," Lianna conceded, "but I am certain that his letter said the box garden."

Philippa sighed impatiently. It was already after midnight and she was afraid that if she were very late for the meeting, Francis might leave, deciding that Lianna had not been able to get away or that his letter had miscarried. "Do you have the letter in your reticule?" she asked, sure of herself but wishing to avoid further argument on the point.

"No," the younger girl admitted. "When I went back to my room to dress this morning, I ripped it into small pieces and threw it in the grate."

"Then I shall just have to trust my memory. The rose garden is not only less exposed and more romantic for a meeting place, it is also in the farthest part of the formal garden very near the road. If he is coming here surreptitously, he would not care to drive up to the door; the rose garden would exactly suit his purpose for both discretion and convenience."

Lianna was unconvinced and the disagreement only heightened her sense of foreboding. "Oh, Pip. Forget this scheme. I cannot like it. I shall find some way of dealing with Francis when he returns to the house, even if it means confiding in Mama."

"There is no need for you to be concerned, Lia," she replied, some of her exasperation showing in her voice. "Please go back up to the supper room. If your mama looks about for either of us and discovers that we both are gone, she may say or do something to cause my absence to be remarked. You will serve me best by diverting her attention away from thoughts of me and implying, if you are asked, that you know me to be somewhere about with friends."

Lianna knew by her cousin's tone that further argument was pointless, so she nodded unhappily, but before she turned to leave, she said, "It is the box

garden, Pip, I am certain of it." But if Philippa heard
her, she made no response and was already half the
distance to the bookroom.

Beyond the box garden, which was to the west of the
bookroom and closest of all the formal gardens to the
house, were the several paths leading to the park and
various other portions of the gardens such as the
topiary, a high-hedge maze that was the delight of
Lady MacReath's guests during al fresco entertainments, and the rose garden. Lianna had seemed so
certain that her cousin had mistaken the place of
rendezvous that Philippa, as she reached the turning
toward the rose garden, hesitated. But the hesitation
was only a momentary thing. She thought it best to
trust her own judgment, and in any case she was
convinced that chosing the rose garden as a meeting
place was exactly what Francis would do.

As she passed along the edge of the topiary, the
exquisitely and imaginatively trimmed hedges seemed
great looming figures in the eerie bluish light of the
moon. To make matters worse, the moon was occasionally obscured by fast-moving clouds and the
sudden changes from moonlight to pitch darkness and
back to light again engendered in Philippa some of her
cousin's foreboding. Under the influence of the dark
garden and the long cast shadows some of Philippa's
conviction that she was doing the right thing and
would successfully carry it off began to melt.

Philippa had visited Lady MacReath's rose garden
on a number of occasions, but tonight the path seemed
endless to her. Even after she came upon the area criss-
crossed with smaller paths and arbors, she saw no sign
of Francis awaiting her on any of the scattered fili-
greed chairs or benches. She went on, deeper into the
garden, and realized that she must at any moment
come to the end of the gardens, which nearly bordered

a lane that led to the road and the main drive of the house.

Philippa began to be less certain of her memory. If it was the box garden to which she should have gone, she doubted her ability to retrace her steps in sufficient time for Francis not to have given up waiting for Lianna. In spite of her anxiety about going on, she had steeled herself to her task and was disappointed at the prospect of giving it up. She made a soft, vexed exclamation under her breath and was immediately startled by a movement near a bush in front of her and a man's whispered voice urging her to come to him. Her heart began beating very fast but all her doubts vanished. She stepped forward and he put out a hand and drew her near to him.

"I'd almost decided you were playing fast and loose with me and given you up," he said in a husky whisper. "We had best be on our way. I think it is going to rain and we should take advantage of the moon while we can."

Without giving her the opportunity of a reply, he tightened his hold on her arm and drew her along beside him at so rapid a pace that they were in the lane before Philippa gathered her wits to wonder what Francis was about. Though she had not expected it, he was garbed similarly in a dark domino that might have been black or even violet like her own; in the shadowed moonlight it was impossible to distinguish color. He was also masked and she supposed that this was yet another concession to discretion. She could not imagine what he was about; she had expected only stolen embraces and romantic blandishments. For one frightened moment she wondered if it were indeed Francis, but a quick glimpse of his fair head beneath the hood of his domino reassured her.

Philippa tried to halt their progress, but she spoke in

an undertone, for she did not yet wish to expose her identity and her protests either went unheeded or unheard. She had imagined him sweeping her into his arms, not into the lane, and she became vaguely alarmed and tried to pull away from him, but she only succeeded in stumbling rather badly and would have gone headlong to the ground if he had not had hold of her. He advised her rather curtly to mind her steps and in the next moment they were at the end of the lane. A post chaise to which four horses had been harnessed stood in the road obviously awaiting them. Philippa was so astonished that she uttered not a word and followed him peaceably enough when he led her up to the carriage.

A coachman sat on the box, the reins in his hand, and a guard held a saddled dark-colored horse by the bridle. Both men turned expectantly toward the lane as they approached and the coachman gathered his horses together as if he expected to be off on a moment's notice. The guard hastened to open the door of the chaise with his free hand.

The scene had every earmark of an elopement and Philippa could scarcely credit what she was seeing; whatever she had expected, it had not been this. She could not even imagine Francis behaving with such shockingly bad *ton*—or with such dash. For a moment Philippa was not displeased. Seeing this hitherto unsuspected side of Francis' character displayed was not unattractive to her, for if she had had any complaint of him before now it was that he was too temperate. But as quickly as she had this thought she recalled that his plan was not for her but for an unsuspecting Lianna, and her emotions turned to anger, disappointment, and something like grief that his attraction for Lianna obviously went much deeper than she had suspected.

None of their meeting was falling out as Philippa had imagined it would, and here, in front of servants, was not the place to play out the dramatic little scene she had planned to enact when she disclosed her identity to Francis, but she now had little choice. She had no intention of taking her masquerade to the point of allowing Francis to carry her off under the misapprehension that she was Lianna. She reached up to pull back her hood and remove her mask, but she was forestalled. She was lifted bodily from the ground by strong arms and gently thrust into the carriage. She cried out in protest as the door shut on her, but again, if he heard her, he ignored her cry. Before she could recover her astonishment or gather her wits sufficiently to open the door and jump down to the ground, the carriage was off and her last sight before they started along the open rode was of Francis leaping agily into the saddle to ride beside the carriage.

Outrage and heartbreak battled for supremacy inside Philippa's breast. She tore off her mask and tried to let down the carriage window to yell to him to make him stop, but even this was against her, for though she undid the catch easily enough, the window came down a scant quarter-inch and refused to budge any farther. There was nothing for her to do but swallow her chagrin and contain her anger, which had no outlet, as best she could.

She had no real concern for her safety. Francis might intend to elope all the way to Gretna Green with Lianna, but the moment he discovered his mistake at the first change, he would doubtless return her to his stepmother at once, much mortified for having his own dastardly scheme come to such a farcical ending. What did concern Philippa was her reputation and what her aunt and Lianna would think when she did not reappear in the ballroom after sup-

per. It was inevitable that Lady Carnavon would inquire for her, which would cause her disappearance to
be remarked. She could only hope that Lianna would
become concerned enough to confide in her mother as
quickly as possible and that one or the other of them
would guess at the truth of what had happened and
think of some means of preserving her name.

Of one thing Philippa at this moment was certain:
however much she might be compromised by this
night's folly, she would not marry Francis under those
circumstances. Hot tears stung at her eyes. It pained
her not only that Francis chose Lianna over her, but
that he did so so underhandedly. She would have been
devastated if he had come to her to tell her of his
attachment to Lianna of his own accord, but what he
clearly planned was to return to Carnavon House
with his marriage to Lianna a *fait accompli*, which
was infinitely more wounding.

Philippa could scarcely wait for the first change so
that she could at least bring this farce to an end, but
they continued on far longer than she would have supposed possible at the breakneck speed at which they
traveled. The horses were obviously good ones, and by
using four instead of two, the load was easier and
could be carried longer. The carriage was well sprung
and the road relatively smooth, but even so Philippa
was bumped uncomfortably about the interior and
was forced to hang on to the strap near the door to
keep from being tossed from her seat.

At last the pace did slacken and she felt a turning
being made, but there was not the comforting clatter
of cobblestones under the horses hooves and the
carriage did not roll to a halt in the courtyard of an
inn. Instead, it continued on at this slower rate,
necessitated by the poorer condition of the road. The

carriage no longer rocked alarmingly, but the ruts were many and Philippa still had to give some of her attention to retaining her seat.

For the first time she began to feel alarmed. They were certainly not headed along the Great North Road for Gretna Green. She began to fear the Francis had something quite other than an elopement in mind for the hapless Lianna, a scheme more sinister than she would have deemed possible for him to concoct or execute, but that would serve his purpose to force Lianna to marry him most effectively without the bother of a long journey and the risk of being over-taken along the way. Where before Philippa had felt heartache, now she was heartsick, and it was nearly a physical thing. How could she have been so deceived in Francis' character? She could only speculate on whether his perfidy extended only to seduction or to outright ravishment.

Her alarm gave away to genuine fear. The simple ruse she had planned for Francis now seemed hope-lessly naive, and in light of the events as they were falling out possibly dangerous. He was prepared to go to such minacious lengths with Lianna, Philippa could only wonder what his behavior would be toward her when he discovered the truth. She had long since abandoned any notion of triumph at meeting him face to face and now regarded it with dread.

The carriage gradually slowed to a walk and finally stopped. Looking out the window, Philippa perceived that they stood before a small house; though larger than a cottage, it was yet not a manor house. Light spilled out into the night from the ground-floor windows and, rather than dispelling the gloom, seemed to enhance it. The clouds had finally suc-ceeded in obscuring the moon, and even as Philippa looked out the window, the first few raindrops streaked across the glass. She had not the least idea where they could be, but of one thing she felt certain: their location was secluded. Nor were the servants likely to be of any assistance to her, for doubtless they were being paid well to be blind and deaf for the evening.

As Philippa's anxiety grew, her imagination took flight. She imagined this new Francis, this man she did not know, becoming overwhelmed with rage at the trick played on him. Balked of his quarry, his own reputation in tatters, he would take his revenge on her, and she could not be sanguine about the form that revenge might take.

The guard had jumped down from the box and was holding Francis' horse while he dismounted. The dark expanse of cloth covering Francis' back seemed to emphasize the breath of his shoulders and Philippa recalled with what ease he had lifted her and tossed her into the carriage. On the opposite side of the carriage there was a holstered pistol hanging near the door, common accoutrement for travelers who ran the risk of meeting highwaymen or other bravos on lonely roads. Impulsively, she slid across the seat and eased the pistol out of its holster. Her domino had a large pocket hidden among its voluminous folds and she quickly put the pistol into it. She leaned back against the squab, her heart beating rapidly, and could not forbear a smile at her melodramatic behavior. However Francis might choose to express his rage and frustration, it was hardly likely she would need a weapon against him, and in any case, she was not even certain that the pistol was loaded.

She put a hand in the pocket, meaning to draw the pistol out and return it to the holster when the door opened beside her and Francis thrust in his hand to assist her. "Come, lovely," he said in a silky whisper. "We've a night of delight ahead of us."

Philippa took a breath and accepted his support; the time had at last come for Francis to learn his mistake. Her head was of necessity bowed as she got out of the carriage, but as she reached the ground, she looked up and then stood stock-still with astonishment. Even in the near darkness she could see that the eyes she looked into were not the serious blue-gray ones of Lord Francis Glennon, but the brilliantly azure eyes of his elder brother, Crispin, seventh Marquess of Carnavon. His countenance expressed a mirror image of her utter amazement.

"The devil," Carnavon exclaimed as Philippa simultaneously cried out in ringing accents, "You!"

The guard still stood nearby with Lord Carnavon's horse and the coachman waited respectfully for the steps to be put up and the chaise door closed. Becoming aware of them and the unexpected delicacy of the situation, Crispin Carnavon said coolly, "Just so. We had best go inside," and suited his actions to his word by taking her arm and again forcing her to move against her will.

As Philippa's surprise lessened, it turned to outrage. She hadn't the least idea how it had come to be Crispin who had abducted her instead of Francis, but her first suspicion was that Crispin was assisting his brother in the intended abduction of Lianna. There was no doubt in her mind now that the moving factor of this plot for Francis had not been Lianna's beauty, but her fat purse; it could only be that if he had managed to convince his brother, with whom he was not always on the best of terms, to become involved; doubtless Francis had agreed to share his booty. At least the dashing behavior that Philippa had had difficulty crediting to Francis was now explained. She had no difficulty at all attributing the planned moonlit meeting and abduction to his brother, whose reputation was not quite so exemplary.

"I have no wish to go anywhere with you," Philippa said angrily, trying to pull her arm from his grasp. "You will take me back to my aunt at once."

"I shall do something quite different if you are not quiet until we get in the house," Crispin hissed menacingly, and dragged her up the stairs and into the house by sheer strength.

The door to the house was opened for them by Collins, Crispin's valet, who momentarily forgot himself to the extent that he allowed his jaw to drop in surprise as Crispin thrust a struggling Philippa into the front hall. "My plans have gone awry, Jem," Crispin said, addressing the servant. "You may serve supper for us in the study and see to it that John Coachman and Wilkins have something to eat. Tell them that my plans have changed and I shall require them to return us to town tonight."

"Tell them that we shall need them to return us to London at once," Philippa said imperiously. "I shall *not* be taking supper with Lord Carnavon."

"That, of course, is your choice," Crispin said in a clipped way. "But we shall not be leaving here until I have had mine; the ride made me damned peckish. You can amuse me while I eat by explaining what the devil you were doing in my carriage."

"I did not choose to be in it," Philippa cried hotly.

He raised his brows in disbelief, and when he spoke, his voice held a hard anger that chilled her a little. "Yet you are here, are you not?" He did not wait for her to reply but nodded dismissal to his valet and turned his back on her, shrugging himself out of his domino, which he cast onto a chair as he passed through the hall. He walked into a room at the far end of the hall, leaving Philippa alone to follow him or not as she pleased.

Philippa had the thought that she could go out the front door unhindered and escape from this place, but since it was now pitch dark outside, raining, and she hadn't the least idea of her location, it would clearly be an exercise in folly to do so. This realization did not create calm resignation in her breast but only greater vexation. She started to remove her domino, felt the weight of the pistol in he pocket, which she had quite forgotten, and decided against removing the domino. She had felt foolish arming herself against Francis, but against Crispin it was another matter. Philippa knew him well enough to realize that he was very angry, however much the veneer of breeding might cover his rage. She recalled some of the unsavory stories concerning his brother that Francis had related to her, and she felt that perhaps it would be wise not to trust Crispin entirely. Reluctantly, she crossed the hall and followed Crispin into the study.

The setting in the study told its own tale. A table placed comfortably near a low-banked fire was lavishly set for two with fine plate and crystal, awaiting only the succulent dishes to be brought by the servants. A prelude, Philippa thought grimly, to the true purpose of the night. The room was dimly lit by a pair of candle branches on the mantel, and in the shadows a wide, inviting chaise longue beckoned.

Crispin was standing by the table, pouring wine into a glass. When he heard Philippa come in behind him, he indicated one of the chairs at the table, but Philippa ignored him. She had no intention of allowing him to see her apprehension. "Where is Francis?" she demanded.

"Francis? In Leicester, I suppose. How the devil should I know where he is."

"You needn't think you can fob me off with lies," she said. "I saw the letter and that is why I am here. I had no notion Francis meant to take it to such an unconscionable length, but if I had guessed you were in league with him, I would not have been as surprised."

"My dear Philippa, you could not possibly be more surprised than I," he said acerbically. "And you, at least, seem to have the advantage of me in knowing what it is we are discussing."

"I think you know well enough. You might as well admit the truth and return me to town at once. You must have realized that the whole of your scheme was in ashes when you beheld me instead of Lianna."

"My scheme is certainly in ashes," he acknowledged caustically. "But upon my honor, I would have been equally astounded if Lianna had gotten out of my carriage instead of you. I was expecting Molly Matlock."

Philippa was momentarily taken aback by this introduction of a new character in the melodrama. "Who?"

"You probably are not acquainted with Molly. She is a connection of Robert Lampray but doesn't move much in the circles you are accustomed to."

"I am not surprised," Phillippa said tartly. "But, pray, what has she to do with Francis' plan to abduct Lia?"

At this point Collins entered the room with a rolling cart laden with covered dishes, apparently not averse to performing the duties of waiter for his master and doubtless well paid for his discretion. Crispin indicated that they would serve themselves and dismissed the valet. "You might as well sit and have a bit of supper," Crispin advised her as he uncovered a dish of lobster patties. "You must have missed supper at MacReath's and standing in the center of the room glowering at me is not going to convince me to return to town one moment sooner than I intend."

"Have you no regard for my reputation?" Philippa demanded indignantly.

His eyes narrowed. "I do. And my own as well. But at this point another hour one way or the other isn't going to make much difference."

Reluctantly, Philippa admitted the truth of this to herself. Unless her aunt and Lianna had the wits to hush up her disappearance from the ball as much as possible, her reputation was already in tatters and returning an hour sooner was not likely to prove a saving grace. The seductive aroma of well-cooked food wafted toward her and tempted her sorely. She was still not convinced that Crispin was not acting on behalf of his brother, for she was not a great believer in coincidence, but although he was clearly quite angry, he did not appear to her to be threatening in any way, and the weight of the pistol in her pocket was no longer a reassurance but just a weight. She shrugged herself out of the domino and cast it onto the chaise and went over to the table, glaring at Crispin when he glanced up at her before she sat down.

With exquisite politeness he offered to serve her from the dish of lobster patties and uncovered a dish of new peas as well. She accepted with equal punctiliousness. Under cover of this commonplace activity she studied her "captor" and reminded herself that it would not do to be off her guard until she was no longer so entirely in his hands.

Crispin had the reputation of being a rake with a long list of broken hearts to his credit. He was undoubtedly an attractive man, with guinea-gold hair that curled naturally into the style known as the cherubim, and eyes of an arresting blue shade that

always seemed to hold a faint light of languid
amusement. But he was no drawling dandy, perpet-
ually sunk in ennui. He was broad-shouldered and
athletically built, a natural sportsman generally
involved in some pleasurable pursuit. He had charm,
too, a gift for address that made him friends wherever
he went.

Although she did not know him well, Philippa had
always liked Crispin, but with eyes for no man but
Francis, she had always been impervious to Crispin's
attractions. Dash was all very well, in her opinion, but
she far preferred a man of steady character. Or at
least, she had always supposed that Francis was the
more responsible of the Glennon brothers. Perhaps he
and Crispin were not so unlike as she had supposed.

Regarding Crispin through her lashes as she feigned
interest in her plate, Philippa had to admit that there
was something faintly menacing in his handsome
features as the candles cast shadows on the contours of
his face. She did not believe this was entirely fancy on
her part, for though he had taken the overset of his
plans (whatever these might have been) with good
grace, she knew that his temper was not always
sanguine and that his anger was more generally
expressed with an iciness far deadlier than heat.

Having taken the edge off his hunger, the marquess
sat back in his chair and sipped at his wine while he
regarded her in a quizzical way. "I truly don't know
anything of a plan to abduct Lianna," he said after a
bit, his tone no longer quite as forbidding. "If you say
that Fran had something to do with it, it must be a
hum. I wouldn't be surprised to hear he'd been making
up to her—she's a lovely little thing with a tidy
purse—but if it's an elopement you mean, my dear
brother wouldn't be guilty of such bad *ton*. Flying in
the face of convention is hardly his style."

Philippa honestly wasn't sure what she thought at this point. She had the unhappy recollection of Lianna's certainty that she was mistaking the place of rendezvous. It certainly seemed incredible that Crispin should have been planning a romantic adventure of his own in the same garden at the same time and that she should have stumbled upon the wrong man. Yet there was something in Crispin's tone that struck her as sincere.

Her doubt showed in her face and he said with a coaxing note in his voice, "Why don't you tell me about it, Pip? We seem to have been cast willy-nilly into a damned delicate situation, and if we are to sort it out and come out of it unscathed, we'd better have it all out in the open."

Philippa agreed, but before she trusted him to that extent, she intended to know more of his part. "Why were *you* meeting that woman—Molly, I think you called her—in the rose garden?" she asked.

Crispin smiled for the first time and the sharp planes of his face softened, making Philippa again aware of his attractiveness. He made an encompassing gesture at the room. "I'll spare our blushes and not recount the details. Suffice it to say that Molly is of a romantic nature and hinted that a midnight rendezvous and an 'elopement' would find her complaisant. It would seem that it was I who was complacent," he said darkly. "The hint of my intentions that I gave her at the ball and the arrangements to meet were quite clear. Since I gather you did not stumble across her on your way into the garden, I can only conclude that I mistook her hints or that she was playing with my affections." His smile suddenly broadened. "Unless *she* ended up being abducted in Lianna's place. Damn dominoes! Everyone looks like everyone else in one."

Perhaps it was the mellowing influence of the food

and wine, but Philippa had no difficulty believing his story. "Francis specifically requested Lianna to wear her violet domino," she said, and told him of the letter and her plan to help Lianna put Francis off for good. She did not tell him of her own attachment to Francis. She had no idea if he had guessed at it as Aubery had, or not, but it was most likely that he had not. Though he had always been civil to her and even kind, Crispin treated Philippa in an offhand way that suggested he took little notice of her beyond regarding her as a connection of his stepmother's. Another woman might have felt slighted that a man so admired by her sex found in her nothing to admire, but Philippa had little more thought for him and so did not look for insult in his neglect.

"Well, that is very like Francis," he said when she had finished. "If he could attach Lia and convince *her* to persuade Charlotte to the match, it would seem less like cream-pot love. Francis would detest being thought anything but good *ton.*"

"Francis was not born to position," she responded, bristling in Francis' defense. "He must make his own way in the world and he cannot ignore the world's opinion."

"It is only reprobate heirs who may snap their fingers at the world," Crispin said dryly. "I have sometimes thought that Francis is envious of my position. I can't think why. I have not discovered in the two years since I have succeeded to the title that there is much more in it than having precedence over most of one's friends at state functions. Certainly he can't envy the fortune that primogeniture has gained me, for my father left me damn near as many bills as he did pounds. Without Charlotte to pick up the household expenses of the London house, I might well have found myself done up at settling day, and more than once."

"I do not presume to know of your affairs," Philippa said primly, unwilling to concede a point in his favor over Francis, "but you do not conduct yourself as a man whose pockets are to let."

He laughed suddenly. "No, I do not, do I? Well," he added with more gravity, "I am scarcely a pauper, but there is nothing in my income to be greatly envied."

"Francis does not envy you."

Crispin's eyes narrowed slightly. "You seem rather well acquainted with my brother's opinions."

Philippa colored slightly. She knew that Crispin had a quick mind, and an unguarded tongue would lead him swiftly to an accurate conclusion of her feelings for Francis. With deliberate casualness she said, "Francis and I have always shared a commonness of thought that has made confidences easy. I admit," she went on quite truthfully, "that I had no notion what he was about with Lianna, but then, if he believed his suit would not prosper if he addressed her openly, he would not say so to anyone, would he?"

"I suppose not," Crispin agreed in such a disinterested way that Philippa congratulated herself for having lulled any suspicion she might have unwittingly stirred in him.

But he was not disinterested in her, not now that she had so forcefully engaged his attention. Philippa's assessment that he had tended to take her occasional intrusions on his life for granted, sparing little more thought for her than he might for an elderly maiden aunt, was essentially correct. It was not that he found her unattractive; his assessment of her physical attractions was favorable. Her golden-brown hair and earnest light-brown eyes complemented her straight, well-formed features. Her figure, now that it was revealed by the removal of the domino, was flattered by the clinging quality of the gray silk. A handsome woman, if not a great beauty, whose looks time would be more likely to enhance than fade. If he had noted little of this before, it was perhaps because his usual taste in women ran to bold beauties, such as Margaret Matlock, and regarding Philippa in the light of a relation, he was not likely to single her out for his attentions (seldom of a proper nature) in any case.

But Crispin spared no more than a passing thought for her unexpected defense of Francis. He was far more concerned with the coil they now found themselves in. They seemed to have been hurled into a comedy of errors, but this was no stage production. There would be a price to pay for this night's folly, and the thought of it was enough to set his features and to cause him to refill his wineglass with enough frequency to attract Philippa's notice.

Francis, when speaking of his brother's more disreputable habits, had hinted to Philippa that Crispin was a hard drinker who only escaped the general repute of being frequently jug-bitten by possessing an uncommonly hard head that allowed him to feign at least the appearance of sobriety when he was quite castaway. Philippa hoped this was true, at least to the extent that he had a large capacity for alcohol, for she feared that, should he drink himself under the table, she would find it impossible to convince his servants to return her to town before morning, and then there would be no help for it; she would face a ruin that was complete and incapable of being suppressed.

She thought of mentioning her concern to him, but experience with Aubery and her uncle had taught her that gentlemen particularly disliked being reminded that they were drinking more than was wise and were likely to imbibe an even greater amount, as if this would in some way prove the want of excess. Instead, she said, "If you have quite satisfied your hunger, I think we had better leave. The time we took to sup may not have mattered greatly, but every hour that passes will make explanations more awkward when we return."

"And just what will our explanation be?"

Philippa opened her mouth to reply and then shut it again. She felt the sudden folly of her masquerade, the absurdity of the coincidence that had led her instead to take the place of a near demimondaine. She sighed. "The truth may seem incredible, but what else can we say?"

"That depends," he said, and got up to pull the bell. When Collins entered a few moments later, he requested, to Philippa's chagrin, not that the carriage be gotten ready, but another bottle of wine. "There is one other explanation that is logical," he said when the valet left them. "What has happened has every appearance of an elopement. We could admit to the tryst in the garden and say that we were caught up in the moment and decided to elope. But common sense eventually prevailed and we returned to do the thing properly."

"That is more ridiculous than the truth," Philippa said scornfully. "In the first place, if we wished to be married, why should we elope? I doubt anyone would object. And in the second place, how would we explain that after nurturing so grand a passion, we have after all decided that we should not suit."

"We don't explain it at all."

The servant reentered the room at this moment with the wine and Philippa contained her response until he had left them again and closed the door. She impatiently waved aside Crispin's offer to refill her glass.

"We would certainly have to do so eventually or we would find ourselves at the altar."

"We would," he agreed in an expressionless way, and taking his glass, he walked over to stare down into the fire.

Philippa did not reply for a moment. "You can't mean that you wish for us to be married?" she said with patent astonishment.

He gave a short bark of laughter that was half snort. "I *intend* for us to be married," he said, glancing at her over his shoulder. "There is certainly a difference."

"I think you are drunk," Philippa said accusingly.

He shook his head. "Not even up in the world yet," he assured her. "I have never known you to be slow of wit, Philippa, and you have been in the world long enough to be past the age of naïveté. If I had turned out to be my cautious, correct brother, you must have found your name in jeopardy for this night's work; as it is, your ruin is complete. My reputation for being in the petticoat line is such that no one would believe you had spent so much time alone in my company and remained virtuous. By taking you from Lady MacReath's garden and bringing you here I have destroyed your reputation past repair, however unwittingly. Rake I may be, but I am no loose fish. If we do not marry, I shall dishonor my own name as well as yours."

"That did not bother you overmuch before," she said tartly.

He turned sharply and she thought she saw something flash in his eyes. But perhaps it was only a trick of the candlelight. "You know of that, do you? My loquacious brother again, no doubt. Then you must see that this time I have to do the honorable thing, or perhaps I should say the thing decreed honorable by the world. My credit might survive one such incident, but never a second."

Philippa pushed her chair away from the table and rose. "This is nonsense, Cris. You don't wish to be married to me any more than I wish to be married to you. I will not spend the rest of my life paying for one night's foolishness. I would rather be ruined."

"You flatter me," he said dryly. "But I was not consulting your wishes in the matter. I was informing you of what must be done whether we either of us care for it or not."

Philippa walked over to the chaise longue and picked up her domino. "I find the prospect of marriage without love insupportable," she said with obvious distaste.

"I begin to sympathize with those who condemn romantic novels for impressionable young women," he said acidly. "Do you realize that our attitudes are reversed? It is you who should be begging me to save your name, and I should be backing away. And you would be well served if I did. This night was not my doing."

"Then I resolve you of all responsibility," Philippa said handsomely as she put on the violet domino. "You need only return me to town and I shall explain everything to my aunt myself, taking most of the blame, if you like. You refine too much upon a few hours; it is not as if we have been gone for the whole of the night. Aunt Charlotte will doubtless be able to squash any bit of scandal that my disappearance from Lady MacReath's may have caused." She tied the strings of the domino and added crisply, "Will you send for your carriage now?"

He was thoughtful for a moment. "No," he said slowly, "I don't think I shall."

Philippa stared at him. "You cannot be serious. If

nothing else, you must wish to allay Lady Carnavon's fears. She must be beside herself wondering what has become of me. If we don't return as quickly as possible, there won't be a shred of honor left for *either* of us."

"I know."

Philippa found him utterly maddening. Francis had told her the story of another woman compromised at his hands whom he had flatly refused to marry, and she could not see why Crispin should do such a volte-face now, particularly as she did not even want him to marry her. He could not possibly care for her, and in many ways they were very nearly strangers.

But it was more than the want of feeling between them that made Philippa willing to risk ruin rather than marry him. In spite of Francis' clandestine courting of Lianna, Philippa knew that in her heart she had not abandoned the desire and belief that this trouble between them would be resolved and they would still be wed. She had every faith in Lady Carnavon, who had great credit in the world, to bring them off from this mess unscathed. She only needed to convince Crispin that he could not force her hand and that the only thing to be done would be to return her to her aunt as quickly as he could. "I won't marry you whatever you may intend," she said with calm assertiveness. "If you will not return me in your carriage, I shall walk to London if I must."

"It is at least fifteen miles," he said with a casualness that made her want to box his ears. "You won't reach town until well into the morning, whether you have an uncomfortable and possibly dangerous walk in the rain or stay here the night with me." He gave her a mocking smile. "Though that, too, may prove dangerous."

Philippa paled. He spoke with the hint of a threat in

his well-bred voice. "You would not dare," she said with more conviction than she felt.

He walked over to her slowly and deliberately. His eyelids dropped over his eyes like concealing hoods and she was not sure she cared for the smile that turned up the corners of his mouth. She stood her ground and met his gaze defiantly, though her heart was pounding rapidly in her breast. In one quick movement he scooped her into an embrace that brought her tight against his chest. The steel she had felt in his grip when he had led her to his carriage was in evidence and she knew well that struggling would be to no avail.

With his free hand he pushed up her chin to bring her lips within reach of his. It seemed a very long moment as their eyes met in a clear clash of unbending wills, but when he at last kissed her, it was not forcefully, but gently and deeply, as if he were making love to her instead of bending her to his will. Philippa had meant for him to find nothing in her but a stony unresponsiveness, and was dumbfounded to feel the flicker of response that coursed through her. By the sudden way his embrace changed to become less binding yet more encompassing, she knew that he had felt it, too. A sudden rush of warmth went through her, though whether it was caused by shame or desire she could not say.

He released her with an abruptness that nearly caused her to lose her balance. His expression was so measuring that hot color stole into her cheeks.

"You see, I would dare," he said, his lips smiling but his eyes cold. "I haven't much taste for an unwilling partner, but it would certainly put a quick end to your refusal to marry me. Don't tempt me with easy solutions, Philippa."

Her heart pumped rapidly and every muscle was

taut. "You will not find it easy, I promise you," she said with scarcely a tremor.

"Nor will you," was his quick response, accompanied by a short, grim laugh. He drained the wine from his glass and put it back down on the table with deliberation. "In what way shall I make you mine, Philippa? Civilized and legal, or rough and ready?"

Philippa was keenly aware of the weight of the pistol at her side, but she was timid of making the motion that might warn him too early of her intention. She certainly did not wish to shoot him, but neither did she have any intention of allowing her will to be broken or herself to be raped. Some little corner of her mind refused to believe he would really do such a thing, but she could not take the chance. She thought perhaps that if he meant to take her into a bedroom, she would find her chance to draw the pistol and keep him at bay. But it was more likely that he would accomplish the thing here on the chaise longue behind her. As stealthily as she could, she put her hand in her pocket and closed it around the butt of the pistol. "If you do not send for your carriage to take us back at once, you shall regret it," she said as evenly as she could.

"Oh, I shall certainly regret this night one way or the other," he said, his eyes touching her in a way that made her color rise. His own color was higher than it had been, and a glance at the table showed her that the second bottle of wine was better than half-empty. The alcohol did not appear to impair him physically in any way, only to make him more menacing and reckless.

Casting caution aside, she withdrew the pistol with as swift a motion as possible, saying, "My brother has taught me how to use a pistol, and if you come any closer to me, I *shall* use it. Ring for your servant."

His blue eyes hardened and she found the faint upturn of his lips chilling. "Now, where can you have found that?" he said almost musingly.

"It was inside the carriage," she replied, seeing no reason to lie. "I presume it is loaded."

"It is."

"Then you know your danger." And she devoutly hoped he did. In spite of her brave words, her knees were beginning to tremble and she did not know how much longer she could keep up a steady front.

"I wonder if I do?" he said quietly, and began to move toward her.

"I am not bluffing, Carnavon." She carefully but deliberately removed the safety catch from the trigger.

He hesitated, but only for a moment. "All my pistols have hair triggers," he said quite conversationally, and continued toward her.

Philippa, seeing that he was calling her bluff, did the only thing she could do: she squeezed the trigger.

3

The retort was deafening in the small room, the smell of burned powder acrid. She had stopped him in his tracks. He stood only a few feet from her, looking perfectly calm, not even his lips parted in surprise. For a moment she half-expected him to sway and fall at her feet, a red stain marring the snowy whiteness of his linen, but after a moment or so he turned away from her, and following his gaze, she saw the shattered wine bottle on the table behind him and the stain that was spreading on the tablecloth.

"Are you that good a shot or that bad?" he asked with no trace of emotion.

"That bad," she admitted, and sank down onto the chaise longue behind her as if her feet would no longer support her.

He came over to her and she looked up at him with fear in her eyes. She had shot her bolt and had no defense against him but her own futile struggles. But he only reached down to remove the pistol from her hand and then returned to the mantel to pull the bell.

Even before he could do this, the door opened without ceremony and Collins came into the room, his usual impassive expression quite wanting. He saw Philippa half-sitting, half-lying on the chaise longue, her face white and pinched, and then his eyes flew to his master.

Without explanation, Crispin walked over to his man and handed him the pistol. "This is from my carriage. See to it that it is reloaded and returned to its holster before we leave."

Betraying no unseemly curiosity even though he had by now taken in the shattered wine bottle and the ruined table linens, Collins took the pistol and then asked Lord Carnavon if he wished him to remove the remains of their supper. Crispin said that he did and requested that brandy be brought when the servant returned.

"If you are going to add brandy to the wine you have already drunk, you may defeat your own purpose," Philippa advised him caustically as she raised herself into a more dignified position.

Crispin smiled and for the first time the expression was genuine and wholehearted, touching his eyes as well as his lips. "Do you know, I begin to think I want to marry you. I would have wagered Doremire that you wouldn't have pulled that trigger; there isn't one woman in a hundred who would have."

The brandy was brought in and he measured out amounts for both of them. He took her glass over to her. She shook her head and he said, "For medicinal purposes. I think we are both a bit shaken."

"You never turned a hair," she said almost accusingly as she took the glass from him.

He returned to his chair at the table. His smile was arid. "I've learned to keep my counsel."

"Would you have raped me?"

"Probably not," he replied with honesty. "I never

thought it would come to that. I thought the threat would be enough to frighten you into compliance. I had no idea you had such bottom."

Philippa rose and walked to the table to put down the glass of brandy. "I am very tired," she said, and her voice did sound weary. "May we please stop playing these silly games and go back to Carnavon House?"

He looked up at her. "Do you agree that we are to be married?"

"If I don't?"

"Then we shall spend the night here. You will be untouched, I promise you, but the world will never believe that."

Philippa felt defeat closing on her, but she was not yet ready to surrender. She supposed she could agree to his demand now and then deny it when they returned to town, but she had her own sense of fair play, and if she was to win this battle of wits, she did not wish it to be by means of subterfuge. He seemed to trust that if she gave him her word she would keep it, and she found herself curiously pleased by this and did not want to violate that trust.

Philippa sat down again in the other chair and a sudden thought came to her. She realized that agreeing to Crispin's demands, even if only outwardly, might not be acquiescence nor dishonesty. She could agree to marry Crispin but the wedding needn't ever take place. She had a vision of Francis being made aware that she was to marry his brother. Though she had defended Francis to Crispin, she knew it was true that Francis was at times envious of his brother, at least to the extent that Francis felt that Crispin attained easily the things he himself had to work for. Even though Francis was playing her false by making up to Lianna, Philippa believed that he did love her. It might be at once a sweet revenge for him to believe that she had chosen Crispin over him, and perhaps also be the push Francis needed to make him realize that if he wanted Philippa he had to come up to scratch now, not in some distant future.

Philippa meant to enlist her aunt's aid to keep as much of the truth as possible from the world in general and Francis in particular. Then, when Francis, realizing that he was about to lose her forever, begged her to jilt Crispin and be his wife, she would convince Crispin to release her from her promise, which she imagined he would readily do. His main concern was preserving their honor, which she believed would be amply satisfied by their announced betrothal whether or not the wedding actually took place; it was not as if he wanted to marry her. Philippa did realize that it might be awkward for her to be betrothed to one brother and eventually marry the other, but she pushed it to the back of her mind as a complication she would deal with later. For now, it was enough to implement her plan.

Philippa stole a glance at Crispin, who was staring into the fire as he sipped his brandy, not seeming to find anything suspicious in her continuing silence. "I shall agree to marry you," she said at last, putting a mild emphasis on the word "agree" and hoping he wouldn't notice. To her mind it was not quite the same as saying she *would* marry him.

He saw nothing untoward in her style of accepting his offer. "Good," he said succinctly, and at last rose to call for his carriage.

Philippa hardly knew why, for this was scarcely a love match or even a marriage of convenience in the usual sense, but she was piqued by his phlegmatic acceptance of her decision, though she could not have said what response she had expected. To punish him,

she did not address him again until they were inside
the carriage and at last on their way to London, but he
appeared to be asborbed in his own thoughts, and once
again her concern was wasted. "There will be no need
to rush the thing," she said when she was finally tired
of hearing nothing but the rattle of the wheels over the
road and the clatter of the horses.

"I suppose not," he agreed. "I should be able to
produce the license by this afternoon or tomorrow at
the latest, but if you wish to buy bride clothes or wait
for Lord and Lady Maverly to travel from Essex to be
at the ceremony, we can wait another week or so."

"I meant that we could wait until we are at
Doremire for the holidays to be married," Philippa
said. "Surely we are neither of us eager for this
marriage."

He shrugged. "Why put it off?" A thought occurred
to him and he regarded her suspiciously at last. "It
won't do for you to cry off, my girl. The gossips will
only be kept at bay for as long as my name protects
you."

Philippa shifted a little against the squabs. "I am
not going to cry off." Or at least not at once, she added
mentally. "But it takes more than a week or two to
have bride clothes made, and you know perfectly how
much my Uncle Henry and Aunt Bess detest coming to
town. It will be much better for them if we are
married from Doremire Abbey."

"Perhaps. But you don't need the better part of a
year to have a few dresses made. We can go to
Doremire at the end of the month."

"I have agreed to your demands, Carnavon, because
you have given me no choice," she said angrily, "but I
will not be pushed into this absurd marriage with
unseemly haste. We shall have the gossips, in whom
you have taken a sudden, unaccountable interest,

watching my fingure and counting on their fingers."

He laughed. "Quite true. But I think you do wish to put off the inevitable. It won't be as bad as you think, you know. You won't find me ungenerous, and if you are discrete—and careful—I won't inquire too closely into the nature of your, ah, friendships."

Philippa was a little shocked at his plain speaking and not best pleased at his complacence. "Perhaps it is you who will be watching my figure," she taunted.

"I said I expect you to be careful," he said with clear warning, and then added in an easier tone, "Let us agree on a wedding at Doremire at the end of the Season, then. That is ample time both for shopping and for resigning yourself to the marriage."

Philippa would have liked a bit more time. She didn't doubt that Francis would come to her, but the more time she gave him to do so, the better. Yet to push Crispin further might make him suspicious. She made no comment, allowing his suggestion to stand.

Crispin's post chaise pulled up in front of Carnavon House not much before dawn; there was already a perceptible lightening in the sky to the east. Most of the journey had passed in silence and both had very nearly drifted into sleep. They were both a bit stiff and rather tired as they descended to the street. Certainly, had it been advisable, neither would have objected to seeking their beds first and leaving tiresome explanations for a saner hour. But there was no choice. The dowager had to be sought out at once, both to put her anxiety at rest and to help them concoct a plausible story to present to the world.

Due to a style of living that frequently brought him home with the cries of the roosters, Crispin carried a key to his own front door rather than have a servant wait up for him indefinitely. They entered the front hall and it was in complete darkness; the first rays of dawn not having penetrated there yet. The house was absolutely silent.

"So much for casting everyone into a pucker," Crispin said in a dry whisper.

Philippa did not care for the implication that no one was concerned at her disappearance and said frostily, "My aunt has too much sense to make a fuss until she is certain that something is really amiss."

"I think losing a niece at a ball is just cause for the vapors."

Philippa did not deign to answer him, but started up the stairs. He caught her arm. It was the first time he had touched her since he had held her in his bruising embrace, and she was intensely aware of the sensation of his hand on her arm. "Gently. We don't want to wake anyone but Charlotte if we can help it." He went up the stair ahead of her and he moved with the careful, silent stealth of a cat. A tomcat, Philippa thought sardonically.

The second floor, where the family's bedchambers were located, was as dark and quiet as the two floors below. Philippa, following behind Crispin, wondered how he intended to wake the dowager without startling her, but his proved unnecessary. As they approached her door, it opened a crack and Lady Carnavon herself peered into the hall.

"Crispin!" Lady Carnavon said, disregarding the hour and raising her voice to a normal pitch. "Thank God, you are home! The most dreadful thing has happened."

Crispin laid a calming hand on his stepmother's arm. "Everything is well, ma'am," he said softly.

"It is no such thing," the dowager retorted with great feeling. She was wearing an embroidered dressing gown over her nightdress, and her black hair, which was streaked in a flattering way with gray, was unbound. It was obvious that, though dressed for bed, she had been awaiting the return of Crispin or possibly had even nurtured the hope that she would see Philippa before the night was out. "Your brother has run off with Philippa, though I am sure I do not know why, and what I shall think of to tell Maverly, I can't imagine. I never would have thought Francis capable of such a thing; he always seemed such a well-behaved young man. Lianna has told me the most shocking things about him tonight and I can only think that I have been nursing a viper in my breast. Now, if you had abducted Philippa, I should not be so astounded, although I must say that I don't see why you would choose to run off with her either—she is not at all the sort of woman to take your notice—but the act is more in your style."

Lady Carnavon finally paused for breath, but before Crispin could forestall a further torrent of words, a sound from behind him in the hall caught Lady Carnavon's attention. "Who is that? Is someone with you, Carnavon?" A darkling thought occurred to the dowager marchioness. "Carnavon, I know that this is your house and that my daughter and I only live here at your pleasure, but I hope you would not dare to offer us the insult of bringing a common woman here while we are at home."

"Only a rather uncommon one," he said dryly, ignoring the unflattering implication to his moral character. "I don't think the hall is the place to discuss this," he added, and firmly ushered his stepmother back into her room. Silently, Philippa followed them.

In the poor light of the single candle branch on her dressing table, Lady Carnavon did not at first recognize Philippa when she entered the room. She was far too shocked at the thought that Crispin had dared to bring home his doxy, and she was scarcely expecting to see Philippa, being quite convinced that for some unfathomable reason Philippa had run off with her other stepson. When Philippa came out of the shadow and close enough for her aunt to see her face, the dowager gasped and clutched at her breast in a dramatic way that was not in the least studied.

To say it had been a very trying night for the dowager would be gross understatement. She was as fond of a masquerade as any young girl could be, but all her pleasure in the party had vanished when her daughter had come to her and told her that Philippa was missing and likely run off with Francis. Lianna was not the most coherent storyteller at the best of times, and in her agitation Lady Carnavon had barely made sense of the story. She could not be made to understand how it was that if Francis had written to plan a tryst with Lianna, he had ended eloping or kidnapping Philippa; even Lianna did not seem to know for certain how this might be, but it was the only thing to account for Philippa's obvious disappearance. Lianna, her nerves worn to a frazzle by the endless wait she had suffered for her cousin's return, feared that Francis had carried Philippa off with nothing short of mayhem on his mind to exact his revenge for their trickery. But Lianna's mother, well aware of her daughter's penchant for lurid gothic novels, had dismissed this flight of fantasy out of hand, supposing that whatever the reason might be, it would not prove so melodramatic.

Affection and her sense of responsibility toward her niece might have convinced Lady Carnavon to raise a hue and cry to try to find Philippa, but her instincts told her that it really was not likely that the girl was in any danger at the hands of her stepson, at least physically. The danger to Philippa's reputation if she raised a fuss was unquestionable.

The dowager had searched the company for her elder stepson, hoping for his advice, only to be met with the information from friends of his that he, too, had not been seen since the time immediately before supper. At first she had found this extremely vexing, but she quickly saw how she might put his absence to good use. Hoping with all her heart that she did the right thing, for Philippa's sake, she made up a tale for her hostess of a sudden migrane for Philippa and implied that Crispin had taken her home in his own carriage. Whtether or not Lady MacReath had believed her, they were old friends, and she would cast no rub in the way of this face-saving lie.

The desperate hope that Philippa would be waiting for them at Carnavon House when they returned was not realized, and so another hastily invented story was conconcted for the benefit of the house servants and Philippa's maid, who had waited up for her mistress's return. But Lady Carnavon knew well enough that no amount of ingenuity or cleverly concocted excuses would save a scandal if Philippa did not return soon. In the morning her lies would be exposed as such and her niece would have no reputation at all left to her.

The dowager had not yet sought her bed, feeling superstitious about doing so, but the truth was that she had had little hope that Philippa would return before morning. But her prayers appeared to have been answered and, as is so often the case, in a way she could not have imagined.

"Pippa, you wretched girl, where have you been?" she said, relief and annoyance warring in her breast. "Where is Francis? Why didn't you send word to Lia or to me if you were going to go off in that inconsiderate way?"

Lady Carnavon collapsed onto the stool before her dressing table and Philippa took a chair near to her.

Philippa cast a darkling look toward Crispin, who had taken a candle from the branch and was lighting others from it. "I could not, Aunt Charlotte," she replied. "I had no notion myself that I would not be returning to the ball."

"I have been nearly beside myself with worry," the dowager complained. "I did not know what to think when Lianna came to me and told me you had disappeared. She was half-weeping and wringing her hands and trailing her court of admirers behind her, none of whom had the least idea what was amiss, but vied for the honor of comforting her. It was all I could do to convince them to leave us, but thank heaven that I did!"

"I gather Lia told you of the trick we were to play on Francis?"

Lady Carnavon nodded vigorously. "And a sillier scheme I hope I may never hear of again. If Lia had told me it was her idea, I might not have been so surprised at its silliness, but it was too complex for her and you were always the clever one. I am not a bit astonished that it all went awry; it could not have been otherwise. Although how it is you are with Carnavon when it was Francis you went to meet, I can't imagine."

"I meant to meet Francis, but I did not. Could not," she corrected with another glance cast toward Crispin, who had deposited his tall frame in a nearby armchair. "I met Carnavon instead."

Lady Carnavon's sigh was almost a moan. "What had he to do with your plan? I shall never understand anything you rackety young people do; it was not so in my day. If we do not end in the middle of a desperate scandal, it will be nothing short of a miracle. And what is most likely is that I shall end in Bedlam before the week is out, driven to distraction with trying to avert ruin."

To put her aunt's mind at rest as best she could, Philippa related, as succinctly and clearly as she could, all that had occurred from the time she had left Lianna in the dimly lit hall at MacReath House.

Lady Carnavon listened attentively and silently, not even interrupting her niece for clarification. When Philippa was through, she gave vent to what was this time unmistakably a moan. "Alone with Carnavon since midnight and with servants who know you both! It is even worse than I imagined. If you *had* been abducted by Francis, it would not be nearly so bad. Maverly will never forgive me; I have promised to look after you and I have violated his trust." She turned to her stepson, who had sat silent through Philippa's recital of events. "Carnavon, how could you behave in such a ramshackle way? I suppose I should not be surprised at it, but I thought you were at least above despoiling members of your own family. At least, Philippa may not be precisely related to you, but she is to me, which must count for something. If your valet or the others should speak to any of the other servants, especially the footman or Philippa's maid, who know that Philippa did not return with us last night, there will be no containing the talk."

"Servants can always be bribed," Crispin suggested.

"A secret shared is no longer a secret," the dowager said with a waspish inflection. "At least when I thought that Francis had abducted Pippa, I had hope that he would realize that he had compromised her and that they must be wed. Now, what is to be done? I can't insist that he marry Philippa just because it was his fault she went into the garden in the first place."

"If Phillippa is compromised, it is I who should satisfy her honor by marrying her," Crispin said.

"You?" Lady Carnavon's surprise was evident. Nor did she seem particularly pleased or relieved with this solution. "I'm sure I don't know what Maverly will say to that; he and Elizabeth have always had hope of a grand match for Pippa, I think, though she is one-and-twenty and the best offer she has had was from Lord Beasley, who was most respectable but hardly a grand match. But then she will not encourage the young men who make up to her, so what else can be expected? I almost think she wishes to find herself on the shelf."

"In that case Maverly may be willing to settle for me," Crispin said with a flat inflection.

Lady Carnavon heard no irony in her stepson's tone. "Yes, he may," she agreed. "You have not got a grand future, but it is an independence and there *is* the title. And though you are a bit of a scapegoat, Carnavon, you are not a hardened gamester or a complete libertine."

"Virtues of omission," he said with an enigmatic smile.

"In any case," Philippa said, "I *am* one-and-twenty and I don't need Uncle Henry's or Lord Tamary's permission to marry. And," she added because she was piqued by her aunt's suggestion that she had failed to attract any eligible *parti*, "if I have not had any 'grand' offers, it is because I have yet to meet a man whom I particularly *wished* to encourage, including Lord Beasley."

"I did not mean to suggest that you were an ape leader, my dear," Lady Carnavon said soothingly, "but this is your third Season and it is not a secret among our friends that your papa did not leave matters as he ought."

"If my principal value on the marketplace is how

much money I can bring to a marriage," Philippa retorted, "then I would as soon marry Carnavon."

"Thank you," said that gentleman blandly but with a faint sardonic curl to his lips. "I might also suggest that you begin to address me by my given name. Addressing me by my title is not suggestive of intimacy."

"Well, we had best make our plans," Lady Carnavon began, her mind moving on to the next problem to be solved. "I suppose Crispin will obtain a special license tomorrow."

"No," Philippa replied. "We have discussed this and decided that it would be best not to be wed with too much haste, for that in itself will cause talk. When it is known we are betrothed, there will be no speculation about my disappearance from the ball and the servants will have nothing to gossip about. There is no need at all for haste, so we shall have the bans called at Doremire in the usual way. We do not plan to have the wedding until the end of June at the earliest."

Lady Carnavon had no objection to this. Immediately she began to think of her nuptials in a positive way, as socially desirable. "In that case, we can announce the betrothal properly and have a ball in your honor. It is a little irregular for both of you to be living under the same roof before the wedding, but I suppose it is unlikely that we can convince Maverly to come up to town and open his house for you, which may be just as well. It is so seldom used that it must be moldering and would likely take an army of servants a month to make habitable. I don't suppose you would care to take rooms somewhere until the wedding," she added, addressing Crispin.

"I would not," he replied. "It *is* my house, as you've pointed out. As long as you and Lia are here, Charlotte, I don't see any difficulty. Your presence must give countenance to us, and in any case, it is less than three months to the wedding."

Philippa wanted to point out that no definite date had yet been set for their wedding, but she was overly sensitive to the fear that Crispin would suspect her motives if she protested too much, especially in light of what she was about to say. "I wish as few people as possible to know the true reason why Carnavon and I are to be married," she said perhaps a little too casually.

"Well, of course, my dear," the dowager said. "If any little comment was caused by your disappearance from the ball, the story that I gave out about you leaving with Carnavon will only be borne out when your betrothal is announced."

"I mean even here, among us. Lianna will have to be told the truth, of course, and I suppose I shall have to tell Aubery at least some of it, for I doubt he would believe that I have formed a sudden attachment or being nursing a *tendre* for Car-Crispin. But there is no reason for Francis to know the truth."

Crispin's expression was sardonic. "You may fool the world, my girl, but you aren't going to fool my brother or anyone else who lives in this house. They know how little mind we paid to each other before tonight as well as we do ourselves."

"He may believe what he likes," Philippa said, but was careful to place no vehemence on her words. "There is still no need for him to know what really happened; if you do not find the circumstance of our betrothal lowering, I do. And it is not as if we have not at least liked each other; if we are only a little more attentive to each other, I think Francis and everyone else will accept our betrothal easily enough."

"If you think I mean to dance attendance on you like a mooncalf for the next few months just to satisfy your vanity, you are fair and far out," Crispin informed her. "I have agreed to put off the wedding to appease your concerns about what the world will think, but make a cake of myself, I will not do."

"I am not asking you to do any such thing," Philippa said with asperity. But it would have suited her very well if he did do just that, for that must convince Francis of the seriousness of their betrothal and perhaps spur him on to declaring himself. "I would not expect you to go out of your way for me," she continued with heavy sarcasm. "I suppose it is enough that you have offerred to marry me."

Her efforts were wasted. He nodded in a brief way and said, "I think so, too." He grasped the arms of his chair and pushed himself upright. "You know best how the matter should be carried on, ma'am," he said to his stepmother, "so I'll leave it to you."

"We shall be sure to inform you of the time of the ceremony so that you can be certain that you are free to attend it," Philippa said sweetly.

"Mind you don't make the notice too short," he advised her with an infuriating smile. He then bid both ladies good night and left a fuming Philippa to animadvert upon his character with greater freedom in his absence.

Lady Carnavon was shocked. "You must not call him an overbearing, impossible man, now, Pippa," she advised solemnly. "He is to be your husband."

"Not if I can help it," an angry Philippa said without thinking.

"Whatever do you mean? Of course you are to marry him. I thought it was quite settled. I know he is not quite the husband I had hoped for you, but in his way he is a very good sort of person, you know: generous, kindhearted, and quite even-tempered, except when he is in one of his black moods and that isn't very often, is it? He is also very well formed and really quite a beautiful young man. And he is, after all, a marquess." Lady Carnavon was ticking off the virtues of her stepson on the fingers of her right hand. As if to make clear the change, she switched to her left hand and began to list his sins. "He does tend to insist on having his own way much of the time," she allowed, "but most men do. And he is rather fond of games of chance, though thank heavens he does not generally play above his means. I suppose you are also thinking of his career among the demimonde, though we should not talk of such things. It may not be a virtue for him to be so attractive with his taste for light-skirts, but then it is not a love match, is it? Even when it is, a woman can never be certain that a man will not stray; it is their nature. It is a cross that most women must learn to bear."

"*I* shall not," Philippa said with a sudden fierceness.

"But, my dear, under the circumstances . . ." She let her voice trail off in a significant way.

Philippa realized that unless she meant to take her aunt into her confidence—and she did not—she had best put a guard on her tongue and behave as though she did indeed accept the fate that decreed she must wed Crispin in a loveless marriage. "I think I am very tired, Aunt Charlotte," she said, suiting her voice to her words. "I know that Crispin and I must be married if there is to be no scandal, and though I would not have chosen a man of his character for my husband, I suppose it could be very much worse."

But the explanation was unnecessary. Lady Carnavon allowed for the very natural confusion of a young woman finding herself in such a predicament. She had never guessed at Philippa's partiality for Francis, for it would never occur to her that her niece would be foolish enough to lose her heart to a younger son whose financial prospects were scarcely greater than her own. "I think we had best take Carnavon's lead and go to bed," she advised. "If you will only think of marrying Carnavon in a positive way," she added with gentle consolation, "you will see that you will come to think of it as a very good thing after all."

"Please let me be the one to tell Lianna what has happened in the morning," Philippa said as she rose. "She will likely blame herself for this and I think I can convince her that she should not." Philippa also hoped to convince her to discretion. She did not mean to confide the entire truth to Lianna either, but she had to convince her that she was not unhappy at being betrothed to Crispin and to get her pledge not to tell any of what had happened to Aubery or Francis. Lianna could be trusted well enough to hold her tongue to the rest of the world, but with her easy, open nature, within the family she was far less likely to be discreet.

4

All of Philippa's careful planning nearly went for naught the next morning. Even with her concern for her cousin to occupy her, Lianna's uncluttered young mind did not find it difficult to drift into sleep, and in any case she had sought her bed some two hours earlier than had Philippa. Philippa had every resolve to be up at her usual early hour, but her maid, believing Lady Carnavon's story that Philippa had remained at the ball with a party of friends and come home later, thought it a kindness to let her mistress sleep longer than usual, and thus Lianna was up and dressed before her cousin.

It was a stroke of good fortune that Lianna, her first waking thought being for Philippa, had dressed as hurriedly as she could and gone at once to Philippa's bedchamber to see if by some miracle she had returned. Lianna did not really have much hope of finding her cousin safely in her own bed. Her delight then at seeing Philippi when she came into the room was such that she gave no thought at all to Philippa's need for rest. She went immediately to the bed and shook her cousin awake. "Pip, you must get up, you wretch. You have given me the most awful fright. Where *were* you? What happened when you met Francis? What did he say?"

Philippa, who had not been asleep many hours, was at first confused by Lianna's bombardment of questions, but as the mists of sleep vaporized, she realized thankfully that Lianna had not yet heard the story from her mother or Crispin, and she willed herself to complete consciousness so that she would have her wits about her as she convinced Lianna to see the situation as she wished her to. Philippa wasted no time on unnecessary preamble. She at once launched into the story of the events of the previous night, backtracking occasionally when Lianna's comments and questions caused her to lose the main thread of her story.

"Oh, Pip," Lianna said excitedly, "I vow I am quite jealous. You have had such an adventure and it is so romantic. Imagine being kidnapped and spirited away by a masked man. At least," she continued, for she was not without common sense, "it turned out to be romantic, for it was only Crispin and not some high-wayman or worse." Her moods were always mercurial, and from excitement, a moment or two of thought brought her to contrition. "Aubery is always calling me a widgeon, and he is quite right. It is not at all romantic, is it? You do not really wish to marry Crispin and it is all my fault that now you must do so. You are a sacrifice to my cravenness. If I had dealt with Francis myself, as I should have, this would never have happened."

Philippa could not quite contain her smile. "You *are* a widgeon! Have you thought that perhaps I shall quite like being a marchioness? It is not as if there were anyone else, you know," she said, lying glibly and surprised at how easy it was to do. "Crispin and I have always dealt very well together."

Lianna shook her head. "You are only saying so to spare me my feelings."

Philippa placed a finger against her cousin's lips and said, "I know what I am doing, and I am happy enough in it. I promise you that is the truth." Which it was, though in a way that Lianna could not know.

Her words were enough to silence the younger girl, but Lianna clearly persisted in believing Philippa a noble victim of circumstance. In fact, it proved much easier to convince Lianna to say nothing of the true events to anyone, Francis particularly. Lianna had no difficulty at all understanding that Philippa would not like anyone to think that she and Crispin would marry for any reason but choice. "Even if you are not in love with Cris, Pip, I know it must make you uncomfortable to know that he would not marry you if he did not feel that he had to."

Privately, Philippa agreed. If she were intending to marry Crispin, she would have disliked reminders of that excessively. But under the circumstances, it hardly mattered. Lianna also agreed to speak to Francis at last and convince him, as Philippa had exhorted her to do, that she would never care for him and that he should cease importuning her to meet him.

Philippa's next challenge was facing her brother. He would never believe that she had cared for Francis as late as yesterday noon and by midnight had formed an attachment for Crispin, and no manner of lie would convince him otherwise. He would doubtless be angry with her for attempting the ruse she had planned for Francis, and upset with Crispin for compromising his sister, however unwittingly. But ultimately Aubery would accept the situation, partly because he seldom questioned the wishes or behavior of his elder sister and partly because he was, as usual, likely to be so wrapped in his own romantic concerns that he would spare little thought for Philippa's. As long as Philippa did not appear unhappy with her choice, he would waste little thought on her affairs.

But having crossed the hurdle of dealing with her aunt and Lianna, Philippa was much more confident than she had been the night before that she would be able to manage Aubery, and even Francis, to her liking. She wondered if Francis had remained in London and would return to Carnavon House today or if he had gone back to his friends in Leicester. It seemed almost odd to her that only yesterday she had been pining for his return and hoping for a letter telling her when it would be.

When she encountered her brother a bit later in the breakfast room, quite alone, she used the opportunity to inform him of all that had occurred the previous night. She did not mention the force that Crispin had brought to bear on her to accept his offer, nor did she mention her motive for finally doing so; Aubery accepted without question that she had entered into the betrothal to save herself from disgrace.

But he was upset with her, as she knew he would be, for masquerading as Lianna to trick Francis. "You've finally come a cropper, my girl," he said pedantically. "I've warned you a thousand times that following some maggoty schemes you'd dreamed up would land you in the suds someday. I only hope you don't find you've made yourself a hard bed to lie in. Cris is the best of good fellows, but he's not the husband any brother would choose for a sister. It may be just as well that your heart isn't engaged; he'd lead you a merry dance, I'll wager, if you were expecting him to dote on you."

"He'll doubtless be too busy rescuing me from my 'maggoty schemes' to lead a dissolute life," Philippa said tartly.

"What about Francis?"

"What about him?"

"Didn't fall out of love in an afternoon, did you?"

Philippa took a piece of cold toast from the rack and spread it with marmalade as an excuse not to have to meet her brother's eye. "Let us say my ardor has dampened," she said aridly. "Of course I cannot stop caring in a single day, but I intend to feel nothing more toward him than I would toward any man who was to be my brother-in-law. My eyes are opened to Francis' character now and I would not, in good conscience, be able to marry his brother, whatever the circumstances, were it otherwise."

"You haven't done very well at the hands of the Glennons, Pip," he said on a gloomy note. "It might have been better for both of us if we'd stayed in Berkshire with Uncle Henry as he wished us to this Season. Cupid has proved a cruel god for both of us."

Philippa laughed. "Oh, I expect that one way or the other we shall both come about. There is no need to be melancholy."

"Pray, why not?" said Crispin, coming into the room. "It appears to be the order of the day. I have just had a word with Lia. I gather she envisions a tedious fate for us. What have you been telling the child?"

Philippa knew he was only quizzing her, but flushed a little with annoyance at the implication that she would have spoken of him or their situation unfairly. "What would I tell her but the truth? At first she thought that being kidnapped was an adventure, but her common sense told her that the result of it was less than happy for us. Unfortunately, she blames herself for having come to me for help in drawing off Francis in the first place."

The family served themselves at breakfast from covered dishes spread out on the sideboard, both to free the servants for other morning chores and to allow the Glennons to share one meal without the conversational constrictions of ever-present servants.

Crispin walked over to the board and began to lift various covers to examine the dishes within. "Lia has somewhat of an excess of sensibility," he said as he peered critically at a dish of coddled eggs. "If we do not encourage her to make us out martyrs, she will get over it soon enough." He finally decided against the eggs and placed a few slices of ham on a plate, taking that to the table and sitting in his usual place at the head of the table.

"I object, though, to your choice of words, Pip," he continued as she handed him a cup of the strong black coffee that he preferred with his breakfast. " 'Kidnap' implies an act of some deliberation, and happiness is a relative term. If we make up our minds to be content in our fate, I expect we shall do well enough." He glanced up suddenly at Aubery as if noticing him for the first time. "Philippa's told you what occurred last night? Good. You aren't planning to ask me to name my friends, are you?" he asked with mock concern.

"Devil a bit! I've no notion to catch an early view of my maker," Aubery replied. "You're a dashed good shot, Carnavon. If you've done Pip a harm, you've not been slow to redress it, and it seems to me that it's as much her own dashed fault as it is yours."

"You are generous, Aubery," Crispin said in a tone that might have been taken as sardonic and that earned for him a swift glare from Philippa. "I am glad you do not dislike the idea of having me for a brother."

"Not in the least," Aubery assured him. "At least you and Pip are free to marry if you please," he added darkly, recalling that the morning mail had again brought no letter from his uncle concerning his own romantic aspirations. "There are those of us still treated as children to be guided by the whim of others."

"You may be unlucky in love, dear boy, but your luck may be in on another matter," said Crispin to deflect Aubery from bemoaning his fate, as Crispin feared he was about to do. He was nearly as weary as Philippa of hearing of the charms of Miss Wright and the trials of Aubery's wooing of her. "I saw Balwick yesterday at White's. He said that he is, after all, of a mind to sell you his team of grays."

Aubery's woeful expression perked up instantly. "Did he, by damn? He's led me the devil's own dance this month and more, not knowing his mind in the matter."

"Then, if I were you," Crispin advised him, "I'd call on him at once before he has a chance to change his mind again. If you're getting a bit short before the quarter, I'll be happy to lend you a bit so you can settle the thing at once."

Aubery was clearly delighted. He informed Crispin that he was a trojan and promptly forgot his own troubles and grievances and those of his sister as well. Barely bothering to excuse himself, he left his half-finished plate to call at once for his curricle and to change for the street.

Philippa and Crispin exchanged an understanding smile. For all his intensity, Aubery was still just a boy flitting from one delight to another. If the prospect of owning some prime bits of blood could so easily cast Miss Wright from his mind, it was unlikely that his heart would be shattered if he were not allowed to tender his suit to her. The shared moment put Philippa quite in charity with Crispin, but the mood was destined not to last.

"Are you still wishful to keep the truth of what happened last night from Francis?" Crispin asked.

Philippa's eyes flashed above the rim of the cup of chocolate she was drinking, but Crispin appeared absorbed in cutting and eating his ham, and if the question was asked in any suspicion, she could not tell. "Yes. The fewer people who know the truth, the better. I wouldn't have told Aubery, either, if I had thought I could make him believe otherwise."

"You think you can convince Francis that it is a love match?" he said disbelievingly.

Philippa's brows knit. She knew what she wanted Francis to think, but she could not share this with his brother. She wished that Crispin would stop questioning her on the matter. "Perhaps he will think that I wish for the title," she said crossly. "What does it matter what he thinks?"

"Why, nothing, I suppose," he said, a little surprised at her tone. "But I thought you were determined to convince the world that it is a love match, or do I misunderstand you?"

"What I do not wish is that the world, or even Francis, for that matter, should know that we are constrained to marry each other. It is humiliating!"

"Is it?" He put down his fork and regarded her thoughtfully for a moment. "No doubt you are right. Perhaps a symbol of my devotion would help convince them of my ardor. Both Francis and the world." He removed an opal ring set in chased gold from the little finger of his right hand and proffered it on his palm to Philippa. When she only looked at him in puzzlement, he reached over and gently placed the opal on the ring finger of her left hand.

The fit was nearly perfect, which at first surprised Philippa a little, but as she watched him fit the ring on her finger, she noticed that the hand that held hers was fine-boned, belying the strength she knew it contained. She looked up into his face and was struck, as if for the first time, by the equally fine carving of his features. She had always thought him an attractive man, but now she agreed with her aunt's assessment. It was more: he was a beautiful man. As she looked up into his azure eyes, she realized she was staring and colored delicately, looking quickly away and snatching her hand from his.

"Why should you give me this?" she said brusquely.

"It would serve you as a betrothal ring until I can have a proper one made for you. There is no family heirloom ring to pass on to you, unless it is this, for it was a gift from my grandfather to my father, and from him to me. But it is no lady's ring."

Philippa knew that he wore the opal most days and clearly valued it. Because there was no tender feeling between them and because she meant to be free of her promise to him, she felt awkward receiving the ring but equally awkward refusing it. "It isn't necessary. I've said I don't expect you to play the eager lover." She was about to remove the ring and return it to him when the sound of voices and footsteps in the hall made her pause and watch the door expectantly. In another moment, Francis, still dressed for travel, came into the room and greeted them in the hearty way of a man returning from a long journey.

Like his brother, Francis was fair, but his hair was more sandy than golden, and though his eyes were blue, they might rather be described as blue-gray. He removed his greatcoat to reveal a tall, slender, but muscular form. He tossed the coat onto an empty chair, inquiring as he did so for the other members of the family. He offered Philippa no special greeting, but this was not unusual. In the presence of others he treated her with no more deference or attention than he would a sister. But Philippa, knowing as she did now, that he spoke the same words of endearment to Lianna in private as he did to her, marveled at his casual behavior before her. She knew that she would not have been capable of betraying him one moment and then facing him the next with equanimity. It strengthened her resolve to see her scheme through; Francis *would* come to her.

"Carnavon and I have news for you, Francis, that we are most anxious to share," she said, suddenly wanting him to know at once. "You are to be happy for us, for I am soon to be your sister."

Francis, returning from the sideboard with a full plate, looked at her with his brows furrowed. "My sister?"

"Your brother has asked me to be his wife and I have accepted." She laid her hand on the table in an obvious way so that he could see the opal, which she knew he would recognize, on her hand. "It is only temporary, of course. A proper betrothal ring is being made for me by Rundell and Bridge, but Carnavon wished me to have something at once." She regarded Crispin with a languishing smile. "He said it is to be a topaz set in diamonds to match my eyes."

Crispin blinked. "Did I? How very romantic!" Philippa's adoring expression was marred briefly by a flash of anger. He smiled. "The topaz to match the color of your eyes and the diamonds the flashes of fire." He turned to Francis. "You *do* wish us happy, dear brother?"

Francis was looking as astonished and little pleased by their news as Philippa could have wished. She could only hope he would not be so affected that he would make his feelings too obvious, for she did not at all wish Crispin to know of their attachment. "Y-yes, of course," he said at last. "But this is very sudden!"

Crispin was looking at his brother in that speculative way that Philippa always found so disconcerting. She found it equally disconcerting now to have him regard Francis so. She was well aware that Crispin would not be an easy man to fool.

"Yes," said Crispin, "It is, but in a way it is not." He looked quite deliberately from Francis to Philippa and back again, making her all but certain that he suspected something between them. From there it would not be a very long way to guessing her intention. "I think, perhaps, that the seeds of our circumstances were planted some time ago," he added cryptically, and Philippa did not dare to ask him his meaning.

Francis seemed to realize that he was ignoring his breakfast and began to cut up pieces of egg, though he made no attempt to eat. "It sounds like you're talking in damned riddles, Cris. Is this serious, Philippa? Are you and Cris really to be married?"

"Quite real," Crispin answered before Philippa could speak. "It has not been announced yet, but Charlotte is aware of it and the match has her complete approval. But your want of enthusiasm, dear boy, makes me fear that you do not approve."

Francis looked uncomfortable. "Of course I approve. Why should I not?"

"I don't know, Francis," Crispin said in his silky voice. "Only you could say."

Philippa was becoming increasingly anxious at the turn the conversation had taken. "You must have been up with the birds this morning, Francis," she said quickly to turn the subject.

"The birds?" Francis said stupidly. He had scarcely absorbed all that he had heard since coming in to the room and did not at once understand her.

"I think Pip means that Leicester is a good three-hour drive from here," Crispin supplied, willing for his own reasons to discomfit Francis. "You must have left with the dawn to be in London so early. Unless, of course, you left yesterday perhaps and spent the night with friends along the way."

"Of course not," Francis said a little tightly, not pleased to have his early arrival remarked on. "I left Leicester this morning by post chaise, but the horses were good."

"That doubtless accounts for it," Crispin said blandly.

Philippa had had no more intent when she had spoken of Francis' early arrival than to turn the subject. But she understood Crispin's quizzing of his brother and was a little afraid of it. No more than she wanted Crispin to know of her feelings for Francis, did she wish Francis to know that she was aware that he had planned to meet last night with Lianna. "What difference does it make?" she said to Crispin, her voice more waspish than she intended.

"You are unaccountably cross this morning, my love," Crispin said chidingly. "You will have my brother wondering at us."

Philippa flushed and Francis said, "Well, I certainly do wonder." He had pushed back his plate, giving up the pretense of eating. But his voice as he spoke was well controlled and expressed no more than curiosity. "A fortnight ago when I left town you never had a second glance for each other."

Crispin looked at Philippa as he spoke. "Attraction is an unaccountable thing."

In her anxious state, Philippa felt nearly certain that he was speaking of her attraction to Francis. If his intention were to toy with her to make her betray herself, she was not going to play into his hands. She pushed back her chair and stood up. "I hope you do not dislike the match," she said to Francis, unconsciously echoing what Crispin had said to Aubery. "I know I shall be very happy to have you for a brother." She said this last with a bright smile for Francis' benefit, and left the room.

When she had gone, the brothers faced each other for a long, silent moment. It was Francis who finally spoke. "You really are to marry Philippa? If anyone else had told me of it, I wouldn't have credited it."

"Why not?" Crispin said. "Whatever you may say, it's plain that you do not like the match. Why, Francis? I always thought you were fond of Philippa."

Francis didn't answer at once. He had not had any conscious desire to wound Philippa when he had turned his attention to Lianna; he simply had not thought of anything beyond his own needs and desires. It was not that he did not think of Philippa at all; in an undefined way he regarded her as necessary to his comfort. Philippa always thought of him. She understood the difficulties and soothed the annoyances of his life. The discovery that she could settle her affection on someone else stunned him a little, and he was even less pleased that her choice was his brother. It was not as if there were any enmity between him and Crispin, but they were not close and there was a definite if public acknowledged rivalry between them. It hurt that Philippa had turned to another; it rankled that it should be Crispin.

Nor was the timing propitious. Francis consoled himself that Lianna had failed him the night before because she had been unable to get away, but not with the same conviction that he had convinced himself that her reluctance to listen to his addresses was mere maidenly modesty. As little as he liked to admit it, Lianna had never given the least encouragement to his pretentions, and he had no reason at all to hope that she ever would.

Now, even the bird he thought he had safely tucked away in the bush had flown away the moment his back was turned. Not even considering his own want of fidelity, he himself felt betrayed. His anger, though, was more directed at his brother than at Philippa. It was less difficult for Francis to believe that Crispin, with his reputation of being so fatally attractive to the fair sex, had cast out lures to Philippa, then to believe that he had lost her affection through any fault of his own.

But it was not in Francis' nature to vent his anger openly. His years of political subservience had taught him the foolishness of displaying raw emotion and the efficacy of manipulation over demand. Nor was he any more eager than Philippa to admit to his brother that there had been an attachment between them. Francis shrugged as if to show his lack of deep concern. "Of course I am fond of Pip. She's nearly as much our sister as Lianna. But of all the women of our acquaintance I cannot think of a less likely bride for you. You're not a man to suffer boredom easily; I should think you'd have your first mistress mounted before the ink is dry on your marriage lines."

"You think Philippa will bore me?"

"Well, she's not much in your style, is she?"

Crispin's eyes narrowed, though his expression and tone remained unaltered. "And what is my 'style'?"

"High-fliers," Francis responded without hesitation. He knew the signs of impending anger in his brother well enough, but he was angry in his own right and did not care. "Diamonds of the first water who have little else to recommend them, including virtue. But then, I expect that is a good part of their attraction for you."

Crispin did not appear abashed at this animad-
version on his character, he only smiled. "You can't
have expected that I would take a light-skirt for my
wife. Not even you would think that I was that much
of a loose fish. But I am not quite sure I understand
where your concern lies; is it for my eventual boredom
or Philippa's dillusionment?"

Francis did not answer the question but after a
moment said, "What can you possibly see in her?" He
sounded genuinely puzzled. "She's pretty enough, I
suppose, but she's no great beauty. She has a mind and
is conversable, but what is that to you? There's no
dowry to speak of—five thousand, according to Charlotte."

"Put like that, one almost wonders," Crispin said in
a dangerously silky voice. "But do you know," he
added, casting out a tentative line, "I rather thought
at one time that *you* had an interest there."

"That's it, isn't it?" Francis said, suddenly abandon-
ing his air of indifference. "You guessed that she cared
for me and you thought you'd see if you could cut me
out. It's just as it was when we were boys: you always
had to ride faster and better, shoot straighter than I
did. Isn't this taking that sort of thing rather far, Cris?
Parson's mousetrap has no exit."

An enigmatic little smile just touched the corners of
Crispin's mouth. The bait had been taken, and his
interest grew by leaps and bounds. He hadn't guessed
at the attachment at all, at least not before this
morning, and he found it more than simply interesting
that Philippa had said nothing to him about her
feelings for Francis last night when he had questioned
her motives for keeping Lianna's rendezvous in the
garden. "The competition between us, dear brother,"
he said, "is largely in your own mind. If Philippa had a
tendre for you at one time, obviously it is behind her.

If it were you she preferred, how could I have succeeded?"

"How do you suceed with every other female who unsuspectingly falls into your snare?" Francis asked with a faint supercilious raise to his brows.

"Never by false promises and subterfuge," Crispin said leadingly, and saw by the martial light that sprang into his brother's eyes that he had scored another hit.

"I made Philippa no promises," he retorted, defensiveness at last betraying him into anger.

"So I gather," said his brother with sardonic succinctness. "But then perhaps that is your 'style.' No matter, your loss is my gain."

"Much good may it do you," Francis said nastily. "As head of the family it should be your responsibility to do what you can to increase our fortune rather than add to the burden by allying yourself with a woman who will bring you little more than her person."

"Is that why you never offered for Pippa?" Crispin asked softly.

"Can I marry where I would?" Francis said bitterly. "I'm a younger son who had a meager legacy and small prospects beyond what I can make for myself."

"Would you have offered for Philippa if she had, oh, say fifty thousand pounds instead of a paltry five?"

"Without a moment's hesitation," Francis replied, not at all aware of the implication of his words. "She is exactly the sort of woman I admire. Great beauty in a woman is nothing more than a superficiality. In a wife one should seek sense and a pleasing nature above all things."

"After first determining her portion," Crispin said. "I quite agree. Handsome is as handsome does." He pushed back his chair and rose, but before leaving the room, he said, "If Philippa so fits your ideal for the perfect wife, you should be condoning my good taste, Fran, rather than condemning it. She may not have a fine portion, but she comes from rich stock. She may yet prove to be a greater prize than either of us ever imagined."

Francis looked up at his brother, a faint sneer marring his handsome features. "Are you counting on Aubery to rectify the inequities of their father's will? There's no harm in him, but he has little thought for much beyond his own comforts or difficulties. By the time he comes into his own, he won't even think of it."

Crispin smiled again in his maddeningly inscrutable way. "Perhaps he won't need to," he said, and left his brother to stare disconsolately into his plate of cold eggs.

5

The betrothal of Miss Philippa Worth to the Marquess of Carnavon was something of a nine-day wonder. Not even Sally Jersey could make herself superior by declaring that she had noticed for some time that Lord Carnavon and Miss Worth had been smelling of April and May. They had never shown each other the least partiality, and it was true enough what Francis had said: Philippa, with her pleasant straight features, honey-colored hair, and uncompromisingly brown eyes, was not the sort of woman who usually attracted Crispin. And given the ephemeral quality of his previous attachments, it was generally supposed that Carnavon had not a heart to lose. Nor could members of the *ton* nod knowingly and say that of course it was an arranged match; neither was the possessor of the fortune that usually went with a marriage à la mode.

Nor was there grist for the mills of those who would have whispered scandal. Lord Carnavon might have the reputation of a rake, but Philippa's credit was beyond reproach. She had never behaved in any way that might have been described as fast, not even to the extent of gilding her toenails or dampening her petti-coats. In fact, after the surprise of the news had worn off, most people assumed it was yet another classic

case of a rake who had reached the time in his life
when he was ready for a comfortable wife.

Philippa, a little to her surprise, found herself the
object of much attention and envy. As Crispin had not
paid a great deal of attention to her before the night of
the masquerade ball, neither had she given him much
of her notice. Accepting the good wishes of her friends
and acquaintances, she discovered that many young
women seemed to think she had managed a great feat
to bring a man like Crispin up to scratch. She was told
again and again how handsome, how dashing, how
charming, was her husband-to-be.

There were times when she found Crispin quite intriguing. One moment he behaved toward her in the
same offhand, brotherly way that he always had, and
the next there was something of the lover in his
manner. Even though her heart was given to another,
Philippa could not help feeling flattered to have a man
so many would not have scorned as their lover behave
as though he found her desirable. Yet, when she remembered the way that he ruthlessly swept her into
his arms that first night, and her own unwilling
response to him, she was glad enough that her heart
was not free to lose to him.

Since Crispin chose to be more attentive than she
had expected, they spent a considerable amount of
time in each other's company, and she found this no
burden, her liking for him increasing daily. He had a
wry sense of humor that could turn quite delightfully
wicked but was never cruel, and the sort of tempera-
ment that could carry him through any situation with
perfect aplomb. Having always viewed Crispin im-
personally with the opinion of the world, she was
genuinely surprised to discover how many views and
ideas they held in common. Despite his reputation, she

could find nothing in his character that would lead her to condemn him out of hand as either a cold fish or a loose one.

But the notice she took of his charms was relatively dispassionate. She never lost sight of the true reason for her betrothal. While she spent greater time in observing Crispin, the majority of her interest was still in Francis. Francis' manner toward her was somewhat remote, but Philippa was not daunted by this; she was delighted. If he did not care for her, why should he treat her differently than he did before? It spoke volumes to her that he had never demanded an explanation of her, and she concluded that the hurt she had dealt his heart made him stand upon his pride so that the wound would not be revealed to her. At least for now. She felt she need only go on in the way that she was toward Francis, pleasant but mildly indifferent, and eventually he would be piqued enough into revealing his heart.

Lady Carnavon might have had a daughter of her own to settle in the world, but she was not at all of the nature that would cause her to behave niggardly toward her niece, and the betrothal ball that she planned was as lavish as any she might have staged for Lianna. All the word was agog with the dashing new poet, Lord Byron, and his first published effort, *Childe Harold*, and taking her cue from this, Lady Carnavon gave the ball an eastern theme. By midday the day before the ball her ballroom had already been transformed into an enormous silk tent with potted palms outlining the balcony doors and tasseled floor pillows cast negligently into corners where chaperone chairs were usually placed.

"The only thing missing is a camel," Crispin commented dryly when he went with her to examine the draping of the silk before luncheon. "Do you really expect any of our guests to recline on pillows between sets?" he asked disbelievingly.

"Of course not," his stepmother retorted. "The pillows are only for show. The usual chairs and sofas will be in place, only hidden a bit by the silk so they do not intrude. Lady Greenway has just redecorated her ballroom in the Egyptian style and is lending me the chairs she has had made, so that should help."

"I hope Lia won't have her nose put out of joint by this," he said. "I should think you'd have a time topping this when her turn comes."

Lady Carnavon gave him a condescending smile for his male ignorance. She left the ballroom to descend the stairs to the morning room, where she planned to make out the place cards for the small, select dinner that would take place before the ball began. It was a chore she enjoyed and always set aside for herself.

Lianna came into the room waving a rose posy with enough force to risk doing violence to the fragile blooms. "Look, Mama, it is from Sir John Trellaway," she said, naming the man on whom her interest was currently fixed. "And the note that was with it said that he would call this afternoon to beg me to save him the first and last dances. Isn't that the most romantic thing imaginable! But that means I shall not be able to accompany you to Miss Denny's this afternoon. I would not wish to be out when he called."

"If you mean to have him, it might be a better idea if you went to Miss Denny's after all," Crispin advised her.

"But if I am not here," said Lianna, examining her posy more carefully in the light coming through a pair of double windows that overlooked the garden, "he will think that I didn't care whether or not he called."

"Exactly," Crispin replied. "But tonight, at the ball,

you eschew all other flowers but those he sent you to carry. When he asks for permission to lead you into the dance, you will say that you are already bespoken for that set, but your eyes should tell him that you wish it weren't so."

Lianna gave up her examination of the rosebuds to regard her stepbrother quizzically. "But why should it be so if he has asked me first? If I stay home to be here when he calls, the whole thing will be set before the ball even begins, and I shall have nothing to regret at all."

"No doubt you are right," he said blandly, but he caught the dowager's eye on him and gave her a quick smile.

"You are a cynic, Carnavon," she said but without admonishment.

"I would have said a realist."

The dowager finished the last place card in her delicate flowing script and pushed herself back from the table a bit to examine her handiwork. She called Lianna to her side to show her the seating arrangement she had made for the dinner, and Crispin, feeling *de trop*, was about to leave the room, but nearly collided with Philippa as she came dashing through the door in the manner of a hoyden, her overdress a bit askew, her hair half coming down on one side. There was something about the delicate color that touched her cheeks and the bright, clear delight in her eyes that made him catch at his breath.

But Philippa scarcely noticed her betrothed. "Aunt Charlotte, Lia, you will not believe it," she said, her voice as excited as her countenance. "It is the most astonishing thing imaginable. My cousin, Lord Tamary, was carried off of an apoplexy." All of a sudden her face sobered, and she added hastily, "That is, I am sorry for Cousin Dominic, of course, but he

never took the least pains to be nice to Aubery or to me
and he even said when he was made our guardian that
it was only a nuisance to him. So he has never
pretended to care for me or pay me the least heed. At
least, not until now."

"I am so sorry, my dear," said Lady Carnavon, and
added in an admonishing tone, "but in spite of his
neglect, you must not sound as if you are pleased that
he has died. He was your kin, after all."

"Yes, Aunt Charlotte," Philippa said as meekly as
she could. But even though she had the breeding to
know she should be displaying at least some sort of
mourning, she could not quite keep the joyous smile
out of her eyes. "But, imagine, it happened a full
month ago. He left instructions that he did not wish
anyone to be notified when he died beyond his
immediate neighbors. He told his solicitor that he
didn't want a lot of false mourning to take place by
people who had scarcely known him and didn't care a
fig for him. He must have meant us, of course. He
always was an odd sort of man."

"It certainly explains why Aubery has not heard
from him," Lianna said. "His letter must have reached
Edinburgh after Lord Tamary had already passed
away."

"And they have only just informed you now?" Lady
Carnavon said indignantly. "Well, I call that shabby
whatever Tamary's wishes may have been. It shouldn't
have been up to him to decide if you wanted to pay
him your last respects. He was one of the last of your
father's family, after all."

In spite of herself, Philippa could not keep her
expressive eyes from dancing. "But Cousin Dominic
has not behaved shabbily toward me in the least. He
has left me the whole of his estate, which was not
entailed and entirely without condition." She waved

several pieces of hot-pressed paper in front of her aunt, who took them from her. While Lady Carnavon looked over the letter, Philippa threw her arms around Lianna and said, "Now we are both heiresses! We shall be positively converged upon by fortune-hunters."

"But you are already betrothed," Lianna pointed out to Philippa, who in her excitement had entirely forgotten the intricate coil in which her life was now entangled. Almost her first thought when she had read the letter was that now there was no obstacle to a marriage with Francis. Philippa turned to where Crispin had been standing when she entered the room in her helter-skelter way, and seemed a bit surprised to find him still there. He was regarding her in such a curious way that she flushed slightly and turned away. She had had the quick thought that perhaps she could solve the problem by simply talking to Crispin, telling him the complete truth and explaining her feelings to him. But she knew as she looked at him that it wouldn't be that easy. And then there was Francis himself: under the circumstances she could scarcely inform him that all was now well and that they could be married after all.

"Perhaps people will say that Cris is a fortune-hunter now," Lianna said archly to quiz her step-brother. "His pockets may not be to let, but he *is* expensive."

Crispin did not answer her in the same light vein. "People will say what they will, whatever the truth may be," he said in a hard voice.

Lady Carnavon's exclamation diverted their attention. "My goodness! Philippa! This lawyer does not write precisely clear—what lawyer does?—but if I understand this correctly, you should receive in excess of eighty thousand pounds. Oh, my dear, only Miss Ledderly is anything to you in fortune this Season. If you were not already bespoken, you would be the toast of the town!"

"Whereas instead, she has already thrown herself away on me," Crispin said in his dry way.

The dowager regarded him curiously. "Whatever is the matter with you, Carnavon? It sounds as if you are not happy for Pippa. Of anyone, you should be the most thrilled of all, next to Pippa herself."

"Of course I am happy for Philippa." He held out his hand to her. "My dear, I could not think of anyone I would rather see have such good fortune. That may sound self-seeking, since you are to be my wife in a short time, but I assure you it is sincere." He removed a small box from his coat pocket and gave it to her. Inside was nestled a beautifully wrought ring with a center topaz set in diamonds. "It is a bit anticlimactic after your news, but I hope it is what you could like."

Philippa had only made up the description of her betrothal ring to goad Francis, and she felt uncomfortable that he had taken pains to have it made to her liking. She thanked him a little shyly, knowing that she took it under false pretenses.

It was not as if they were marrying for any of the usual reasons or even by choice, and Philippa understood that he for quite different reasons might feel a bit awkward, too, now that she was an heiress, about having forced their betrothal. "No one supposed you were hanging out for a rich wife, least of all me," she said with a laugh. Yet, in some curious way, she was not displeased that Crispin, whatever his reasons, had been willing to marry her with no thought to a portion. Francis had certainly thought of it. But Crispin, after all, had the title and a competence, if not a fortune.

The dowager became concerned about the fate of

the ball planned for the very next evening, thought of all her wasted work and what a wretched mess it would be to cancel it at the last moment due to Philippa's bereavement, and decided it would be best to think on the matter before taking such a step. Philippa agreed that, under the circumstances, it would be a shame if the ball could not go on, but agreed to be guided by her aunt's decision in the matter.

The thing that most marred her pleasure in learning of her good fortune was that she could not share her news with Francis. He had left early in the morning to attend a cockfight at Horely and had not said for certain whether he would return to town in time for the ball. He had not said that he did not wish to be present at her betrothal ball, but Philippa inferred that that was his reason. Francis might accept her approaching nuptials, but he would not be hypocrite enough to celebrate them. This did him no harm in her eyes.

She wondered what would be his reaction when he learned of her good fortune. She could even imagine some of Francis' chagrin when he heard of the prize he had let slip through his fingers. She could not quite like the idea of her money being a lure for the man she loved, but again she excused any mercenariness in Francis as the product of necessity.

By that evening she had woven a hundred fantasies of what her life would be like with Francis now that they would have the money to live in some style. As an ambitious young man with a fortune behind him, now he would doubtless find a seat where he could stand as candidate, and have the ready he needed to give any incumbent a run for his money. Then he would no longer be a hanger-on to the great men of politics but one of them.

Philippa quite decided that Francis would be a member of Parliament before the year was out and saw herself as an admired political hostess and avid campaigner for her husband's seat. À la Georgiana, Duchess of Devonshire, she would personally visit the voters of Francis' district and offer them smiles and kisses in exchange for their votes.

Philippa half-expected that Aubery would be envious of her good fortune, since his own future was so unsettled at the moment, but he was delighted for her. "Damme, Pip, I think it's of all things famous. Though," he added gloomily, "I'm likely to suffer for Tamary's eccentricities. I know Hobarth is screwing up his couarge to speak to Lydia, and by the time I can draft another letter to convince Uncle Henry to approve the match on his own, it may be too late."

"But Uncle Henry is a more liberal guardian than Cousin Dominic," Philippa pointed out, "and without that influence will be likely to give you your head in the matter."

Aubery brightened at once. "Devil a bit, you may be right. The truth is," he added a bit shyly, "I meant to make up for Papa's wrongheadedness as soon as I could. I never saw it in him myself, but he must have been getting dotty to have left things the way he did."

"Aunt Charlotte told me that our mama was shockingly expensive when she and Papa were first married," Philippa confided as she settled herself comfortably in one of the large leather chairs in the library. "She said that it caused a deal of trouble between them. I don't think Papa held much store by putting money in a woman's hands."

"Then he might as well have made arrangements to put you in a convent," Aubery said. "What the devil sort of future did he expect for you?"

"Since there was no hope of my finding a husband without a large dowry?" Philippa said dryly.

"I didn't mean that," Aubery assured her. But he added, "Well, it did make it impossible for you and Francis, didn't it? What happened there, Pip? Both of you seem to go on as if nothing untoward has happened, and you behave as if you don't mind in the least that you are to have one brother instead of the other. You ain't the fickle type."

"Like you?" she said quizzingly, and earned a rueful, self-mocking smile from her brother. She would have liked to confide in her brother, but was not sure she could trust him to see the matter as she did. Being a man himself, he would likely side with Crispin and think it unconscionable that she used him to get to Francis, even though Crispin's heart was no more engaged than her own. And yet she longed for the solace of a secret shared. "After what Francis did, letting me believe that he cared for me and then arranging trysts with Lia, he needed to know that there could be someone else in my life," she said in reply to his question.

Aubery closed the book he had been reading when Philippa interrupted him and put it on a table next to his chair. "I don't suppose you had much choice in marrying Crispin. If there was any talk about your disappearance from MacReath House, it didn't reach me, but you may depend on it, if your betrothal hadn't been announced the next day, there might have been a scandal. But it would be best if you resolved any feelings you still have for Francis. It won't be a comfortable thing for you once you are Lady Carnavon if you are wearing the willow for your husband's brother."

"I shan't be," Philippa said with assurance. She could not resist at least hinting to him of her intention.

"But Crispin and I are not married yet. Now we must even set the date back for six months as I shall have to be at least in half-mourning for Cousin Dominic until then. Who knows what may transpire by then?"

Aubery's eyes narrowed suspiciously. He studied her face as if he were reading her purpose clear on it. "You are up to something," he said definitely. "I hope for your sake that it isn't another of your maggoty schemes. Unless Carnavon is playing a willing part, Pip, you'd best have a care. He won't much like being a pawn in some game you're playing."

His reaction was what she had feared it would be, and with a sigh she gave up any idea of making him a confidant. "Don't be absurd, Aubery," she said, managing to coax a tone of wounded virtue into her voice.

"I know you've something in mind," he insisted. "A fortnight ago you were wearing your heart on your sleeve for Francis, and now you act as if it is a matter of indifference to you that you're to marry Cris instead. It don't wash, dear sister."

"Indeed it doesn't," Crispin said behind them, and they both jumped as if caught out in some misdeed.

Philippa, her cheeks stained crimson, scrambled to her feet, feeling at a disadvantage looking up to his greater height. "You must have come creeping upon us, Carnavon," she said a little tartly. "It was most uncivil of you to interrupt us in such a startling way."

"My manners are not always as they should be, I fear," he said. Turning to Aubery, he added, "You should know, dear boy, that the heart is not always obedient to the will. I seem to recall that Miss Brandon held your heart at Christmas when you were visiting Doremire. But it is Miss Wright who now has that honor, is it not?"

Coloring a bit, Aubery agreed that it was. Though Crispin spoke lightly enough, Aubery could see that there was a hard light in his eyes, and he guessed that Crispin had not cared for the remarks he had overheard. He didn't know how much Crispin knew or suspected of Philippa's feelings for his brother, but there could no longer be any doubt of them now. He felt a little guilty that it was his fault she would feel his wrath, but not guilty enough to remain to assist Philippa in the discomfiting scene that he suspected was about to take place between his sister and her betrothed. Excusing himself rather hastily, he left Philippa and Crispin to face each other.

Philippa, not one to cry craven in a difficult situation, began with a frontal attack. "You must wonder at what Aubery has said."

"Not really," he said evenly, but she could sense anger lurking below the surface. "What I wonder at is that *you* did not see fit to tell me of your interest in my brother."

Little flickers of fright teased at her, but she could not think why. Crispin might now guess at her reason for agreeing to the betrothal and doubtless he would be angry, but what of it? If he washed his hands of her and ended the betrothal at once, it might alter her plans, but since she did not mean to marry him in any case, it didn't really matter.

He stood a few feet from her and his eyes seemed unblinking, never leaving her face. The usual pleasant light that made his eyes so attractive was replaced by a hardness that now made them appear like cold blue steel. As her foreboding grew, she recalled Aubery's warning that Crispin could be a dangerous man to use. Her discomfort grew, but she would not admit to it; she would not let him place her at a disadvantage. "It was no concern of yours," she said haughtily. "It is not as if I wished to marry you or you me, for that matter."

"On the contrary," he said, "it is every concern of mine, whatever my wishes may be. You shall find me even less easy to fob off than Aubery. I want to know what you are about, Philippa. Now."

"How dare you take that tone with me," she cried, indignant. "You are not yet my husband to order me as you please."

A smile played on his lips that she found faintly chilling. "I never dared hope for meekness in you, Philippa," he said, his voice at its silkiest, "but I expect honesty in you and sufficient loyalty not to cast me in disgrace either publicly or privately."

"You insult me, my lord," she said evenly.

"And you insult me, Philippa, if you think me obtuse. You might have trusted me with the truth about Francis. It wouldn't have changed anything, I suppose, but it would have made matters between us easier. I find the fact that you did not tell me, shall we say, interesting. You do not dissemble or have a taste for the romantic subterfuge like so many of your sex. If you did not tell me, you had a reason. I want to know it."

Phillippa had forced herself to meet his gaze squarely so that he would not guess at her inner perturbation, but now she dropped her eyes from his and turned a little away from him. "I didn't know how to tell you," she said in a less martial tone, belying his assumption that she did not dissemble. "I could not think of a way that would not be awkward at best, and the longer I put it off, the more difficult it became. I *did* have a *tendre* for Francis, I admit. That was the real reason that I took Lianna's place that night. I wanted to teach him a lesson." She looked up at him again for a moment and then studied the pattern in the Turkey carpet. "As you say, it doesn't change our situation, so what purpose is served by your knowing?"

"You don't feel that it places me at a disadvantage that you admit to an attachment for my brother?"

Philippa looked up, surprised. "But you and I have never pretended that there is feeling between us. You are not at all the sort of man I would wish for a husband."

"And what manner of man do you admire? Francis?"

She turned away again and walked toward the windows. "I am not as certain of that as once I was," she admitted, and realized with a bit of a start that it was true. "But I know what I do not want in a husband. I don't want to stay awake nights wondering what bed my husband is sleeping in; nor do I wish to have to ward off the advances of my husband when he is castaway or to worry over whether the money for the tradesmen will be lost in a night of play in some gaming hell."

He came toward her slowly. "You think that is the sort of husband I would be?"

"Wouldn't you?" She turned to face him.

He stopped, again only a few feet from her. Their eyes held for a long moment. "My reputation precedes me again, or should I say supersedes me?" he said bitterly. "When was the last time you saw me stupid with drink, or losing more than I could afford gaming, or flaunting my mistresses in the faces of my family."

Philippa was not prepared for the vehemence of his defense. "I—I didn't—"

"Yes, you did." He laughed sardonically. "But then, you do have a tendency to take people at face value, do you not? You have done the same with my brother."

"You have little cause to be jealous of Francis," she

retorted. "He has not had the advantages in the world that you have enjoyed."

"I quite agree, but I am envious of the splendid character he is given with little apparent effort on his part. I am as easily condemned on the basis of gossip and malice."

He spoke without obvious heat, but she sensed that he was excessively angry. Angrier than she thought the situation called for. She felt it showed another side of his character she could not quite like: jealous vituperation. "Francis is nothing like you," she said, and her tone made the words an insult.

"What do you really know of my character, or of Francis'?" he said in a level voice. "You come to us for a few months out of the year and see the social masks we put on for guests. What you know of us you know by hearsay and incomplete observation."

His words had the uncomfortable effect of making her feel an outsider. Stung, she lashed back. "If it is hearsay, then it is widespread. Everyone knows what you are; for every one person who wished me well of our marriage, two hoped that I would not regret it."

"I doubt that it will be you who will regret that night's work."

Angry tears stung at her eyes and clutched at her throat. She wanted to tell him her own reading of his character with no influence of hearsay, but she could not trust herself to speak without dissolving into angry tears, so she contented herself with fixing on him her fiercest and most fulminating stare. It had no discernible effect on him.

"Did you suppose that your interest in my brother would be a matter of indifference to me?" he said, and now she could see the fury lurking in his eyes quite plainly now. "I wish no less than you that we had not been brought to this pass, but we have and we *shall* go through with it. But mistake me not, Philippa. I can scarcely forbid you to know Francis without making a scandal of it, but I can and I will prevent both of you from handing me my horns."

He was not an easy man to catch off guard, but she managed it. Her hand came up with a swiftness that surprised even her, and she struck him full in the face. The sheer, blazing anger that was displayed in his eyes in response to her act made her back away from him, as if she feared retaliation. But he only put his fingers to the spot on his cheek where the clear outline of her hand still showed.

She felt the window at her back and recalled only too well the power and ruthlessness of his embrace. Her heart was beating wildly and hot furious tears stung at her eyes. She was a little afraid of him, but her own anger was such that she could not will herself to speak reasonably. "Do you think I would marry a man who had such an opinion of me? I don't care what the world will say. If I am ruined, it is a better fate than being your wife." With these words she moved quickly away from the window. She nearly ran to the door as if she suspected that he would forcibly prevent her from leaving. The door stuck a bit and she struggled to open it, a sudden panic coming over her. She looked over her shoulder half-expecting him to prevent her escape, but he made no move to do so; in fact, he watched her in a dispassionate way, a faint sardonic smile playing on his lips. Feeling a little foolish, she pulled all the harder at the handle and at last the door came open and she was nearly cast into the hall. Fortunately no one was in the hall to see her odd behavior. When she reached the service stairs at the end of the hall, she paused for a moment to gather herself together and then ran up to her room.

Once there, she abandoned herself to tears that were

part anger, part self-pity, and part disappointment. All of her pleasure in her inheritance had been destroyed by her encounter with Crispin. She meant what she had said to him, and she considered their betrothal at an end. This should have given her satisfaction, for it freed her to be with Francis as much as her inheritance removed the obstacle to her future with him, but it did not. Her spirits were woefully depressed.

6

When her aunt came to her to tell her later in the day that she had decided that the ball should go on and to discuss a few last-minute details, Philippa had long since dried her tears, but she could not quite bring herself to tell the dowager the truth as she had planned. That the ball being given in her honor was pointless, in any case, because there would be no wedding. Philippa convinced herself that she did so to spare her aunt the upset that she would doubtless feel. And it was not as if she had really intended to marry Crispin in the first place.

Crispin was not at home to dinner that night, and whatever his engagements for the evening, he put in no appearance at the rout that Philippa attended with her aunt and cousin. But the next morning he made a point of seeking her out.

There was no longer anything forbidding in his aspect. "I am sorry, Pip," he said simply. "I should not have spoken to you so."

"It doesn't matter," she said coldly.

"It matters very much. We shan't jog along very well in harness if we are forever at daggers drawn."

"I meant what I said. I won't marry you, and the world may say what they will of me."

The hardness returned swiftly to his eyes, but then he smiled and said pleasantly enough, "Come with me to my study, there is something I wish to say to you."

"You won't change my mind," Philippa said firmly. He said nothing, but held out his hand to her and after a moment, almost against her will, she took it.

He led her to the wing chair near the grate, but did not sit himself. For a long moment he said nothing, but there was something pensive in his manner, as if he were trying to decide just what he would say. "You do not wish to ally yourself to someone of my unsavory character," he said at last, "but what do you really know of me?"

Philippa was a little startled by this beginning, for it was not what she had expected him to say. "You are a rake," she replied. "They say that you change women the way that most men change coats. I have heard that you will do anything for a wager, that you will spend any amount on your pleasures, and that you drink to excess."

"*On dit*," he said, with a soft but unmistakably sardonic laugh. "Who says this, Pip?"

A faint color came into her cheeks. "Everyone," she claimed defiantly.

"Does Charlotte say it?"

"She would not. She is very fond of you."

"And I of her. Do Lord and Lady Maverly say it?"

"Uncle Henry does not approve of gossip," she said repressively.

"It is strangers, then? I own myself a little surprised that anyone outside the family would discuss my behavior with you—it is such an ill-bred thing to do— or that you would so readily listen."

"Of course I would not listen."

"I didn't think so," he said with satisfaction. "Then, it must be Francis, there is really no one else, is there?"

"He does not disparage you," Philippa insisted. "He has confided in me his concern for the manner in which you conduct your life and has sometimes deplored that you did not behave more responsibly, but he has never condemned you."

"No, he just draws the lines and allows you to fill in between them."

"You don't like Francis, do you?"

Crispin shrugged. "Let us say I do not care for the way *he* conducts himself. Did he tell you the whole of the story, or was he content to see me damned with half-truths?"

"You do him an injustice," Philippa said angrily.

"We shall see." At last he came over to a chair near her own and sat. "Now you shall hear the root cause of my bad character. Ten years ago, when I was just about Aubery's age, I, too, fancied myself in love and thwarted in my honorable intentions. The particulars don't matter beyond that she was a few years older than I and a widow, respectable enough, but yet dashing enough to skirt social censure. I wanted more than anything in the world to marry her, but I was under age and my father would not hear of it. An elopement to Gretna Green was a possibility, but she wanted a proper wedding. I decided to force my father's hand. I compromised her in such a way that the only hope of salvaging honor for either of us was for us to be married, and at once." He paused for a long moment and Philippa half-wondered if he meant to go on.

"My father was furious, of course, but I didn't care for that," he said at length. "I'd had a special license in my pocket for a sennight. But it turned out that the lady was hedging her bets. There was someone else with a place in her affections and in her bed, and I only discovered it the day before the wedding was to take place." As he spoke, his voice became increasingly colorless, as if he feared displaying any emotion. "I tore up the license and wished her well of her lover. In retaliation, she went to my father, claimed to be carrying my child, and swore that in her ruin she would drag our name through the mud as well. My father sent her to the devil but she did her work well and we were the *on-dit* of the Season that year. I was sent to relatives in Cornwall to weather the worst of it, and it did turn out that she was quite discredited through her own doing, but mud sticks, and my character remained tarnished as well. I shall not pretend that this affair was the only folly of my youth, but it cast all my affairs into the light, so that even the silliest excesses of my salad days are now imbued with a more sinister quality."

"What happened to the child?" Philippa asked.

"There wasn't one," he said with no discernible bitterness, and smiled with self-mockery. "Even if there had been, I knew it wasn't mine. I was a noble youth in those days."

Philippa, always able to feel for the plight of someone else, readily saw in her mind Crispin as a very young man, desperately in love with a beautiful but heartless older woman. She saw him not as the dashing, self-assured man she knew now, but as a vulnerable boy used and crushed at the hands of an unconscionable light-skirt. "You must have loved her very much," she said gently.

His response to her sympathy was to laugh. "Not at all. It proved to be calf love that a good dose of reality completely cured. Its only lasting effect was to give the world an opinion of me that was only partially deserved. If I am completely honest, I suppose I must admit that there have been times when I have lived up to my reputation out of sheer perversity, but I don't believe I am particularly imbued to vice."

"But she must have hurt you dreadfully, at least at the first," Philippa suggested, unwilling to abandon her romantic depiction of Crispin as a young man in the throes of his first love.

But he would have none of it. "Gammon," he said with bald flatness. "Most people fall in love and then fall on their faces at one time or another. It was little more than that. If anything, I was grateful, even then, that I had learned the truth before vows had been exchanged and I was forced to live my mistake for the rest of my life."

Philippa was not entirely sure what she thought of the story he had told her. But she did not doubt the general truth of it, for, except for the particulars that absolved Crispin of blame, it was basically the same story that Francis had told her. "Perhaps I have been guilty of judging you without knowing all of the facts," she said. "But knowing them now, it certainly makes me wonder why you would want to marry me. There is no love between us, and this is just as likely to be a mistake that you will live with for the rest of your life."

"Actually, my dear Pippa, I don't particularly want to marry anyone; it has nothing at all to do with you. But marry you I must, and precisely because of the events I have just related."

"That is nonsense," she said. "What happened ten years ago has nothing to do with us."

"It has everything to do with it. If your name were sullied at my hands, what do you think would be said this time?"

"That would surely be more my concern than

yours," she replied. "If I am willing to risk my credit, I don't see why you should feel obliged to force on us a marriage that we both find repugnant."

He gave vent to a short, exasperated sigh. "There are times when I am sorely tempted to leave you to the fate you seem to crave, but *my* name would not stand a second scandal so reminiscent of the first. It is not nearly so much nobility that makes me insist as it is pure self-interest. I would have no honor at all left to me."

"At least you are honest," Philippa said tartly as she rose.

He looked up at her and smiled. "Would you want less? But I do care about you, Pip. I don't wish either of us to be hurt in any way." Then he said so abruptly that she was startled, "Do you really so prefer Francis to me?"

She felt that more than vanity prompted the question, but his expression told her nothing and she could not gauge his humor from the tone of his voice. She decided to answer with the unvarnished truth. "Yes," she said succinctly. "You don't like that, do you?"

As if her words had struck an unexpected chord, his eyes instantly shuttered. "No," he said shortly, and just as abruptly stood. "Be that as it may, in a few months' time you shall be my wife, not his. Make up your mind to it, Philippa, I won't release you from your promise." With this, he turned on his heel and left the room, closing the door behind him with a little bang.

There were any number of minor details that wanted seeing to before the ball began that evening, and Philippa knew she should be helping her aunt, but instead she sank back into the chair and, placing her elbows on her knees, cupped her chin in her hands. She was not entirely sure why, but she felt terribly confused. She also did not know why she trusted the veracity of what Crispin had told her, but she did. What difference did it ultimately make that Crispin was not the libertine she had thought him? It was only Francis' character that should matter to her.

Yet she was pleased enough with matters as they were, for she was sure that Francis was inwardly upset at her betrothal, however well he might seem to take it on the surface. Though she understood the pride that would forbid him to speak to her of it and thus show his vulnerability, she would have liked it far better if he had ranted and raved and called her faithless when he had learned she was to marry Crispin. At times it seemed to her that since the day she had read the letter he had sent to Lianna, she had become increasingly aware of aspects of Francis' character that she could not entirely like. Philippa did not care to think that Francis had deliberately wished her to be misled about his brother; she could think of no motive for his doing so that was not distasteful to her. She forced herself to recall all that Francis had told her concerning his brother, and in honesty she could not recall that he himself had ever uttered a disparaging word against Crispin other than to tell her these things that were not to Crispin's credit. Crispin was right, she had supplied the judgment. Perhaps the fault was hers and not Francis'. If Francis had not told her the complete truth, she was sure that it was because he had not known it himself. He was five years his brother's junior and would probably still have been at Harrow in those days. One did not discuss such things with children, and as the brothers were not close, it was not likely that Crispin had ever confided in Francis.

Having come to such a satisfactory conclusion, Philippa left the study and went upstairs to find her aunt. The result of this interview was that she was certainly in better charity with Crispin, but none the less determined to find herself the wife of his brother before the year was out.

It had taken considerable soul-searching on the part of Lady Carnavon to decide that it was proper for them to go on with the ball in spite of Lord Tamary's recent demise. She was loath to call it off when so much preparation had already gone into it and the time to give notice of its cancellation to all of their friends was impossibly short. The thing that finally convinced her to continue with their plans was the odd behavior of Lord Tamary himself. It had been his own choice that his family members not be permitted to pay proper respect to him. If they had learned of his death at the time, a full month earlier, the ball would never have been planned, or if the letter from the baron's firm of solicitors had arrived only two days later, it need never have been a concern.

She came up with what she thought to be the perfect solution. The old lord's passing would not be formally announced until the following day, and Philippa would have to put off sharing her good fortune with her friends for another day or two. The dowager was a realist, though; all the inmates of the house were aware of the truth and inevitably so were a number of the servants, so it was quite possible that some hint might escape. Other members of the *ton*, hosts and hostesses themselves, would likely understand her decision to go on with the ball, but it was wisest not to give them unnecessary means for censure.

She convinced Philippa to put aside the lovely rose-colored gown she had had made especially for the ball and to wear instead another recently made dress of lavender silk that might be considered at least half-mourning, should anyone ever look to condemn Philippa for a want of proper feeling toward her departed uncle. Lady Carnavon agreed with Philippa that it would only occasion talk if she did not dance but convinced her niece to restrict herself to country dances and to eschew the more elaborate cotillion and the dashing waltzes.

With a small sigh, Philippa saw the rose silk and a number of other gaily hued gowns of fashionable design put away in tissue paper at the back of her wardrobe. The whims of fashion being what they were, she wondered if the dresses would still be presentable by the time she would be allowed to wear them again. But the thought made her feel guilty. Perhaps she had never known her Uncle Dominic well enough to truly grieve at his death, but he had thought enough of her to leave her the largest portion of his estate, and if nothing else, she owed him her respect and gratitude.

As Philippa had expected, the Maverlys had sent their regrets that they could not journey to town to attend her ball, though they professed themselves happy with the match and wished both Philippa and Crispin the best in the world. Philippa had been happy enough that her Uncle Henry and Aunt Tess had decided against coming, for she knew how much they disliked traveling and visiting London and she did not want to discomfit them unnecessarily, especially as the betrothal was a lie. But she found herself longing for thier comforting hominess, and at least she would have had someone in whom she could have confided and shared her delight at her newfound wealth.

Generally pastels and insipid colors did not become Philippa, yet when Philippa's abigail, Susan, twitched the folds of lavender silk, trimmed delicately with lace, so that they fell perfectly about her slim figure, Philippa had to admit that the image reflected back to her in the cheval glass in her dressing room was quite elegant. She was very well pleased with the effect and only regretted that Francis would not be there to see her looking so well.

Lady Carnavon was a favored hostess among the cream of the *ton*, for she spared no expense for the comfort and entertainment of her guests. All the dictators of good *ton* were present, including the revered and sometimes feared patronesses of Almack's and even the great Beau Brummell condescended to put in an appearance. Sarah Jersey, who never missed a good party, was one of the first to arrive and would be one of the last to leave. Marie Sefton, generally held to be the best-hearted of the patronesses, made a point to engage Philippa in a full half-hour of conversation to make it clear to the world that she favored the match. And she advised Philippa, in a way that somehow managed not to be impertinent, how best to manage a husband in general and one who was a reformed rake in particular.

Without Francis present to see her basking in the congratulations of her friends, it was all sadly flat, particularly as this was not really the celebration of a triumph as everyone supposed, but only a sham. She stood up for the country dances with various friends and listened to the sundry comments and social platitudes of her guests. She replied to them with equal insipidness and felt the entire entertainment was utterly vapid. She was aware that she was out of humor this evening, though she was not certain why. Perhaps it was because of her uncle's death, or more honestly, because she could not share the good fortune of her inheritance. Or it might have been nothing more than a simple regret that this ball was for her and Crispin instead of her and Francis.

She deftly managed to avoid participation in the forbidden dances with the assistance of Crispin, who dutifully engaged her at these times so that it was in no way commented on. At one point as they sat with Lady Carnavon during a waltz, Philippa thought he looked as bored as she, and she commented on it.

"No. How could I be?" he said languidly. "It is our betrothal ball." She favored him with a warning glance toward the dowager, but he only smiled. "Actually I have been admiring the Carnavon diamonds. I'd forgotten how lovely they were. You don't wear them often, Charlotte."

"I've never had much fancy for jewels," the dowager marchioness confessed. "But since you are to marry Pippa and they will soon be hers to wear, I thought I might as well wear them at least once more, and this seemed a suitable occasion. I hope you will like them, my dear," she said to Philippa.

"They are very beautiful," Philippa responded, but like her aunt, she had no passion for adorning herself with stones.

"Well, if you're going to be that tepid about them, I might as well sell them and use the profit toward my next settling day at Tat's."

Lady Carnavon flashed her stepson a look of concern. "I hope you are not in difficulties, Carnavon," she said.

Philippa thought his smile was a little frigid. "Nothing over which I shan't come about," he said without disquietude and immediately turned the subject, which Philippa thought might have meant that he had no outstanding debts or that he did not wish to discuss those he had.

Crispin remained obediently at her side for much of the ball, but eventually they were separated into different groups during conversation. Philippa saw him later leading an attractive young matron into the dance. The young woman looked up at him with a

saucy and, to Philippa's mind, inviting smile, and
Crispin appeared to respond to her in a way that must
have given the lady satisfaction. It could hardly
matter to Philippa that other women found him
attractive or that he should return the admiration, but
this was hardly the time or place for it and she was
exceedingly annoyed with him. She then lost sight of
him for quite some time so that she very nearly
accepted an invitation to take her into supper from
another, when he suddenly appeared again at her side.

"Where have you been?" she demanded a bit
crossly. "I have scarcely set eyes on you in the last
hour."

"Not yet wed, and a shrew already," he commented
with a smile. "I wasn't sure that you wished me to
remain with you all night. It is shockingly unfashion-
able to be in each other's pockets."

"Since this is *supposed* to be our betrothal ball, it is
insulting to me for you to have half the other women
in the room languishing on your shirtfront."

He opened his eyes wide at her exaggeration. "My
dear, it is no such thing!"

"You were flirting with Lady Vernay in the most
obvious was imaginable."

He smiled suddenly. "Lettice Vernay is a very old
friend. You refine too much upon it."

"You should rather hope that Lord Vernay does
not," she said waspishly, and took the arm he offered
her as they made their way out of the ballroom.

"I am really quite touched that you are so concerned
for my welfare," he replied.

"I am more concerned for the gossips."

"Ah, yes. The magpies without which no society
gathering would be complete. No doubt they have
already told you that I lost a hundred pound in the
card room tonight."

"I might have guessed!"

"In that case, this conversation is quite super-fluous," he said with maddening sweetness.

A number of tables, seating about six at each, had been set up about the room. Crispin deposited Philippa at one that was already occupied by Sir Aubery and the dowager Lady Carnavon, and then left to procure plates of food for himself and Philippa.

Her aunt chattered happily about the progress of the ball, the number of guests that filled her rooms, and the lamentable character of some of these, but Aubery took little part in the conversation, sitting looking quite disconsolate for much of the time. Lord Henry Cheviot, a persistent admirer of the widowed marchioness, returned to the table laden with food for himself and the dowager and Crispin soon joined them as well, but Aubery made no attempt to visit the buffet and inquiry only elicited the comment that he was not at all hungry.

This behavior was so out of character for her brother that Philippa gave him her attention and realized that he was giving his attention to a table diagonally placed from theirs, at which were seated Lydia Wright, her parents, and a young man that Philippa finally recognized as Lord Hobarth. Miss Wright appeared to be in great spirits. Her conversation was quite animated and she giggled volubly at every comment made by the attentive young baron. Philippa caught her brother's eye and he gave her fierce look, daring her to comment unfavorably upon his beloved. But it occurred to him, before they had returned to the ballroom, that he had never noticed before how high-pitched was Miss Wright's laugh or how quickly he seemed to find it grating.

When it was nearly time for the orchestra to begin playing again and for the company to return to their

revels, Crispin escorted Philippa back to the ballroom.
But before they could reach the ballroom, they were
made aware of a small commotion in the hall near the
stairs. They and others leaving the supper room looked
curiously in that direction but it was Crispin who first
realized what was going forward and Philippa heard
him curse under his breath. Then she saw the
Carnavon butler, Johnson, and Francis appear over
the rise of the stairs. Johnson was clearly admonishing
Francis in some way and Francis was equally
obviously delivering him a set-down. After her first
rush of pleasure at seeing that Francis had come to the
ball after all, she wondered what could be causing
argument between him and the servant and was
shocked and displeased that they should do so in front
of their guests. But then she saw Francis sway ever so
slightly and noticed that his usual immaculate dress
was a little disheveled and she became aware of his
condition.

Crispin started toward them and Philippa would
have followed, but he laid his hand upon her arm to
prevent her. "I'll manage this," he said curtly, and
because she feared a scene, Philippa allowed him his
way. He went over to Francis; they spoke quietly for a
few moments and then disappeared into an anteroom
adjacent to the supper room.

Philippa did not know how many others had noted
Francis' unexpected return, but those that had had the
breeding not to comment on it at least in her presence.
Young men did drink to excess at times, and though
regrettable, it was nothing to make scandal of. Later,
when the dancing had begun again, Lady Carnavon
came up to her niece and said that an old friend of hers
had said he had seen Francis in the hall. She asked if
Philippa had seen him and why he had not joined their
company.

Philippa was forced to tell her of his condition. "I am afraid he was a bit up in the world, Aunt Charlotte," she said euphemistically.

"You mean he was foxed?" asked the dowager, surprised. "Francis seldom drinks more than a glass or two of wine with his dinner. Now, if it were Crispin who were castaway, I should not wonder at it. I have heard that he often drinks more than is good for him."

"Well, it is Crispin who is sober tonight," Philippa returned with a shade of tartness. Almost without being aware of it, Philippa had been watchful of the behavior of her betrothed in the last fortnight, and except for the night of the MacReath masquerade ball, she had not seen him drink to excess on even one occasion in this period, despite the claims of his family that he drank to excess, which she had always taken for granted to be true. The dowager left to see for herself that her younger stepson had returned and in less-than-perfect condition.

The company had thinned out a bit as a number of people chose to attend more than one social event of an evening, but Lady Carnavon's rooms were still comfortably filled and would be so until well into the early hours of the morning. Lianna, who had been sought after not only by Sir John Trellaway, but by a number of eligible and attractive young men, was flushed with her success and a constant round of dancing and insisted that her court leave her in peace while she spent time in conversation with Philippa, who had also decided to sit out the next dance and whose partner was off to fetch her a glass of lemonade.

Lianna joined Philippa on a small sofa in a corner of the room, half-hidden by the draped silk. "I feel as if I have danced the soles out of my shoes," Lianna complained happily, "and I would as lief rest for a bit with you than with Mama, who will doubtless protest that I have shown too much partiality for Sir John."

"Have you?" Philippa asked. "Do you wish for a declaration from him?"

Lianna shrugged her pretty shoulders. "At times I think I do, but then I am not at all certain."

"Be certain," Philippa advised her, "as much as you can. Pretty speeches and romantic airs are not lasting. You would not wish to marry a man you could not regard."

Lianna regarded her for a moment and then said in her direct artless way, "But you do not love Crispin and yet you will marry him. Have you never found a man that you could love? Have you given up trying? Is that why you do not mind that it shall be Cris?"

Philippa did not at all care for these questions and was wondering how she could evade answering without snubbing her cousin when she saw Aubery approaching them, a glass in hand.

"I have this for you from Linington, whom you sent to fetch it for you," he said, handing his sister the glass brimming with lemonade.

"Well, I must say it's shabby for him not to bring it himself," Lianna said with indignation for the slight to her cousin.

"Carnavon didn't give him the choice," Aubery said with an appreciative smile for the memory. "Ferreted out without seeming to do so that he was fetching the stuff for you and managed to draw him off as prettily as you could hope to see. Never said a hard word to him or made the least jealous noise, but I fancy that's one that won't try set himself up as your cicisbeo."

"My cicisbeo!" Philippa was outraged. "That's absurd! Linington is my friend, and I alone shall have the choosing of my friends."

"Don't rail at me," Aubery advised her. "Take it up with Carnavon."

"You may depend upon it," Philippa said, a martial light in her eyes.

"He ain't in anyone's favor tonight," Aubery commented. "Francis just said something about Carnavon getting above himself playing head of the family."

"Francis?" said Lianna. "Is he here? I thought he did not mean to return from Horely until tomorrow."

Philippa's heart sank. Though Crispin had successfully drawn off the hapless Lord Linington, he had obviously failed with his brother. Philippa knew well that Francis was unused to drink and could only hope that his behavior would not be such to cast himself and perhaps the rest of the family into disgrace. On the other hand, though, she could not help but feel a little exulted by his sudden appearance, even in his inebriated condition. She took both as a compliment to herself; that he could not stay away, despite the pain seeing her accept the congratulations of her friends would cause him, and that he was drunk because it was the only way he could get through the ordeal.

But Aubrey apparently saw nothing untoward in Francis' behavior. He shrugged. "Changed his mind, no doubt. He must have come in since supper, I didn't see him before that."

"You saw little of anything but Lydia Wright since the ball began," Lianna said with unaccustomed waspishness. "I wonder you are sparing us a moment away from her."

Aubery raised his quizzing glass and surveyed her in a way that would have discomfited many people, but Lianna did not flinch. She met his grotesquely magnified eye with complete equanimity. "I'd best have a word with my aunt," Aubery said severely. "You're becoming dashed pert."

But Lianna remained unimpressed. "Mama thinks you're making a cake of yourself over that silly Lydia Wright, and so do I," she informed him.

Aubery responded in kind and they were well on their way to a full-fledged squabble, but Philippa made no effort to mediate; she scarcely noticed any of their exchange. She decided that the next move in the game of wits she was waging with Francis was hers, and it would behoove her to seek him out. She left her brother and cousin, and her leaving was scarcely attended.

Even if the company had thinned a bit, it proved no easy task to find Francis quickly. Encountering Lord Vernay as he left one of the card rooms, she asked if he had seen Francis, and was told that he had only just left the card room, although he had not engaged in any of the play. She thanked him hastily and started away but Lord Vernay, a large avuncular man with a dissipated countenance and breath that always exuded spirits, took hold of her elbow and quizzed her in an overfamiliar way about her approaching nuptials. His behavior was certainly worthy of a set-down, but perhaps because she had formed something of a dislike for his dashing young wife and felt sorry for him that Lady Vernay should be such an accomplished flirt, she bore him for several minutes before she made good her escape.

Another friend met in the hall informed Philippa that he had recently seen Francis entering one of the small anterooms adjacent to the supper room. She thanked him hastily, not wishing to find herself caught a second time. Philippa's luck was in, and Francis was in the room talking in a small group to a few of his friends. Only his voice could be heard and the others regarded him with obvious interest.

"Of course he knew she'd come into the old man's money," Francis was saying. "Haven't a doubt of it myself. Carnavon is scarcely all to pieces, but the family coffers aren't what they were in my father's day. He may not have been hanging out for a rich wife, but he couldn't afford to marry with no thought to a portion any more than I could."

One of the gentlemen facing Philippa nodded sagely and opened his mouth to speak when he espied her and turned crimson. His startled, staring expression caused Francis to turn around, but he showed no dismay when he beheld Philippa. "Ah, Pip," he said amiably, his voice only slightly slurred. "It seems I must applaud your good fortune in more than one way tonight. My stepmama informs me that you are now a bona fide heiress. I wonder you are keeping it so close."

"We did not wish to spoil everyone's pleasure in the ball by announcing the *un*fortunate demise of my uncle," Philippa said repressively.

"I'll wager the news didn't spoil everyone's pleasure," Francis said with a knowing smile cast to one of his friends, who looked embarrassed for both himself and for Francis.

"If you are speaking of Carnavon," Philippa said icily, not caring what the other men thought of her words, "*he* behaved just as he ought." With this, she turned on her heel and left them. In the hall she saw Crispin coming out of the very next room, and seeing in him a convenient vent for her agitated feelings, she said angrily, "I thought you were going to deal with Francis."

Crispin seemed a bit startled to behold her but said

in an even tone, "I could scarcely lock him into his bedchamber. He proved to be not only foxed but recalcitrant as well. It didn't help that he met Charlotte in the hall and that she told him of your inheritance. He took what I thought was a rather uncommon interest in it. The best I could do was force him to give me his word he wouldn't have anything stronger than lemonade for the rest of the night."

"I don't think he kept his word."

Crispin shrugged. "And I am not his keeper."

All at once, Philippa's anger, which really had nothing to do with Crispin, left her, only to be replaced by a sick disappointment as she realized the full import of the things she had overheard Francis say. She did not understand how Francis could speak with such disrespect for her feelings and such obvious malice toward his brother. It was absurd and hateful for him to have implied that Crispin had only offered for her because he had known of her inheritance; she herself had known only yesterday. Doubtless Francis was very hurt by her betrothal, but she had not suspected that he would behave with such childish malevolence. What anger she could still muster was transferred to her aunt for being so indiscreet as to confide in Francis when he was obviously in no fit condition to behave as he should.

Crispin saw the change in her expression. "What is it, Pip?" he asked solicitously.

Philippa did not intend to tell Crispin what Francis had said, for she did not wish to add to the fuel of animosity between the brothers. "I think I am just feeling a bit tired. It has been such a full day and it is quite late. I think if I sat quietly for a few moments I would be well enough." Because it was nearest to her, she started into the room Crispin had just left.

He caught her by the arm. "Perhaps I should take

you to Charlotte, if you are not feeling quite the thing," he suggested.

But Philippa had no desire to rejoin the company just yet. She only wanted a few moments to think. "No, I simply wish a private moment. There is no need to alarm Aunt Charlotte. There is nothing at all the matter with me." She started to move away from him but he still held her fast. She looked up at him with surprise. She caught him dart a quick glance toward the open door and she shrugged him off, going into the room with a quick step before he could again detain her.

Sitting on the sofa in the center of the room and blushing quite rosily was Lady Vernay. The gown she wore gave some justice to a growing reputation for being a bit fast. The bodice was cut daringly low, and when she rose, it was quite obvious from the way the folds of silk clung suggestively to her voluptuous form that her petticoats were dampened.

Philippa's hand flew to her mouth in surprise and she uttered an astonished and utterly inadequate little "Oh!"

"Lady Veray was seeking my advice on the purchase of a pair for her new phaeton," Crispin said quickly and smoothly. He was a noted whip whose equipage was complete to a shade and the envy of half the bloods in town, but Philippa turned on him a scathing look that said precisely what she thought of this excuse. But her breeding was as ever to the fore; she would not make a scene that would have the *ton* gossiping for a sennight. "Of course," she said with a smile as false as it was sweet. "And who better to do so? It is well known that Carnavon is a fine judge of good flesh."

"Horseflesh," Crispin corrected mildly.

It is doubted that Lady Vernay heard any of this exchange. Her discomfort and anxiety were patent. Vernay might be considerably older than she, but he was not an old fool. A celebrated beauty with dubious connections and little portion, she could afford no scandal that might cause her husband to put her aside. She murmured something barely coherent about searching for her husband, thanked Crispin for she scarcely knew what, and fled the room.

Crispin, a look of somewhat rueful amusement on his countenance, stood facing his betrothed, who regarded him with icy anger. "Do you know that I was nearly taken in by you this morning? Such a touching story," she said scathingly. "Poor Crispin a victim at the hands of a scheming hussy. Is that one of your standard ploys with my sex?"

"Not at all," he replied, unperturbed. "It was the simple truth. I suppose you do not believe that I was advising Letty Vernay on the confirmation of horses?" She did not deign to answer this and he sighed. "Nevertheless, I was doing just that. You should try to curb this tendency you have to form hasty judgments." He paused and then said in a speculative way, "But if it had been dalliance, would it much matter? You did say that you had no interest in my affairs."

"I haven't," she said frigidly. "Nor have I any intention of marrying a man who would make a fool of me at my own betrothal ball." With this she turned on her heel, but he caught at her arm and with considerable force whirled her about to face him.

He pushed the door into the hall shut before she could reach it and then advanced upon her until she had backed herself against the wall. The by-now-familiar steely glint was in his eyes. "I wonder which of us will end the fool in this? You threaten to end our betrothal every third minute because you have no real intention of going through with it. Do I surprise you?

Did you think me too much of a slow top not to realize your game? I may have played the fool for a woman once; it won't happen a second time. I know you don't really believe it yet, but make no mistake, Philippa, you shall be my wife."

Philippa's heartbeat thudded in her ears and she was aware of the slight feeling of exhilaration that sometimes accompanies fear. "You are right," she said, forcing up her chin to meet his eyes squarely. "I never wanted to marry you. I would rather spend the rest of my life walled in a convent than be touched by one such as you."

A faint smile that held absolutely no mirth curved his lips. "Really?" No more than a foot separated them and he closed this gap so that her breasts pushed against his chest. In spite of a rising panic she refused to give into the indignity of scrambling away from him. "Yet the last time I held you in my arms, I fancy you felt something quite different." Color suffused her cheeks and he laughed, increasing her discomfort. "My dear, what can I have done to cause you to under-estimate me so? What a very poor excuse for a libertine should I be if I were not sensitive to the smallest response in my prey."

"It is your conceit that imagined it," she said fiercely.

"Do you think it might be that?" he asked, his voice taking on a silky quality. She saw what he was about and turned her face away from him, but he caught and held her face in his iron grip and she could not evade him. To her horrified dismay once again she was nearly overwhelmed with the sensation of intense anticipation. But this time she had herself in better hand and steeled herself to no outward response at all to his touch.

When he lifted his lips from hers, an odd smile

played upon his. "Perhaps I was mistaken," he said quietly. "Yet I don't really think it."

Her breasts rose and fell rapidly and not entirely with anger. "You believe what you wish to believe," she spat at him.

He laughed again. "So do you." He released her. "Shall we call this hand a draw, my dear? In our own ways we have each bested the other."

"I think it is you who are castaway, not Francis. The world must be upside down when I find myself tied to you instead of to a man of principle."

"Such as my dear brother, whom you hold up to me as a pattern card of manly virtue?" he said with a faint sneer. "Yet I think I might have persuaded him against joining the company if Charlotte had not happened upon us as we were ending our discussion. I told you he was quite taken by the news that you are now an heiress. It had its effect."

Philippa became suddenly tense. "What do you mean?"

"I think you may know," he said shrewdly. "When I met you in the hall a few minutes ago, you were obviously upset. My dear brother has a carrying voice."

So her discretion had been unecessary. Crispin knew what Francis was saying. She felt a sense of dismay, as if his knowledge of it made Francis' transgression greater. "Francis is drunk," she said defensively.

"Francis is chagrined. He has let an heiress that he might have had for the asking slip through his fingers."

"Your calumny against your brother does you no honor."

"And his against me?"

Philippa opened her mouth to again remind Crispin of his brother's condition, but it sounded a poor excuse now even to her. "You are both behaving so stupidly," she said angrily, "that I wonder if it is not hereditary."

"Do you think I might pass it on to the children we shall have?" he asked provocatively.

She could not help herself, she blushed. Because she could think of nothing to say to him that would not just continue the argument endlessly, she turned on her heel and left him, but as she passed into the hall, she heard his mocking laughter behind her and she felt weighted with angry frustration. Whatever might happen with her and Francis, she had to free herself from Crispin as soon as she could. Every conversation with him turned into confrontation, an endless battle of wits and wills.

The word of her inheritance, thanks to Francis' indiscretion, was spreading about the room like a blaze. As soon as she entered the ballroom, a small group of people near the doorway hastily ended a hushed conversation. Surely this was not meant to be pointed, but it was. It was only a matter of time before someone lacked the breeding or discretion to speak to her about it, and eventually this did happen when no less a person than Silence Jersey took Philippa aside and said that she had just heard of her good fortune and that she would, of course, do nothing to further the news. Philippa was hard-pressed to keep her countenance at this, and as soon as she could, she escaped and found her aunt, who was sitting in a corner of the room (on a comfortable chair, not a pillow) flirting in a decorous way with one of her many admirers.

"My dear, you do not dance?" she said when she beheld Philippa approaching her. "Mr. Danvers was just this minute searching for you to stand up with him for the dance that is forming."

"I met with him a moment ago and begged him to release me from my promise," she replied for the benefit of her aunt's friend. The compelling, commanding gaze she bent on the dowager had its effect, though, and Lady Carnavon sent the gentleman away so that she could have private conversation with her niece.

"What is it, my dear?" she asked the moment they were alone. "You are looking like a thundercloud. That is no way to be on the night of your betrothal ball. It will set people to talking."

"They are doing that anyway," Philippa said. "You told Francis of my inheritance." It was part statement, part question, part accusation.

"Yes," she said, obviously thinking nothing of it. "He is family, after all. Do you know, he did not seem to be quite himself. I think you are quite right that he is foxed."

Philippa cast her eyes heavenward. "Yes, he is," she said with exasperation, "and he has made every person here who will listen a present of my news. That is why I feel it is best that I don't dance any longer. It was well that we decided on the lavender gown."

"I told you how it might be," replied the dowager marchioness sagely, apparently taking no blame to herself for the outcome.

"It is worse than that," Philippa said, not sure why she was choosing to tell her aunt the whole. "Francis has been saying that Crispin knew all along that I would inherit from my uncle and that is the reason he has offered for me."

"Oh! He would not!"

"I heard him say it," Philippa said quietly. "I think Cris has heard it as well."

"Oh, dear," said the older woman, obviously distressed. "There is no saying what a man will do under the influence of spirits."

Philippa liked that excuse for Francis' behavior

when she heard it coming from her aunt even less than when she had said it herself, and said so.

"Yes," Lady Carnavon said, "I know it should not be an excuse for poor breeding, but sometimes it is so. It is nonsense in any case; Carnavon could not have known before you did yourself, and you were certainly astonished when you read the solicitor's letter."

Try as she might, Philippa could not ignore Francis' spiteful behavior, or the reason that Crispin had suggested for it. "I think I am getting the headache," she said dejectedly. "I wish this wretched night were over. I begin to wonder if I shan't regret my inheritance as much as I do this preposterous betrothal."

Lady Carnavon looked quickly about them to see who might have overheard this remark. "My dear, you must not say such things!" But neither reproach nor appealing to her breeding could persuade Philippa to alter her feelings or her willingness to express them.

7

The only reason that Philippa was able to get through the remainder of the evening with some degree of equanimity was because she managed to avoid both Crispin and Francis successfully. Though she was certain she would not sleep at all when she at last sought her bed near dawn, exhaustion, both physical and emotional, quickly overtook her and she slept well beyond her usual hour the following morning.

In the bright light of a sunny April morning, it was easier to reflect on her problems without becoming utterly cast down by them. Crispin had infuriated her last night and Francis had gravely disappointed her. She did not know that even the extenuating circumstances of alcohol and rejection could excuse the latter's behavior last night; from the former she expected nothing other.

Francis had not only insulted her, he had not even had the grace to seek her out to apologize for his behavior. The things Crispin had said to her might have caused her to harbor murderous thoughts toward him, but at least he played his cards faceup. She might dislike their confrontations but she knew where she stood with him. A thought, quite unbidden, came to Philippa, causing her to wonder what it would be like if her betrothal to Crispin were one of choice. But she immediately shrugged it off as nonsense.

Lianna and Aubery, with the buoyancy of youth, had been the first to arise that morning, and by the time that Philippa went down for her breakfast they were on the point of leaving for a drive to Richmond. "Aubery is using me as duenna," Lianna said darkly. "Lady Wright would only allow Lydia to drive out with him for such a distance because he told her that I should be going as well."

Philippa was amused by the glare they exchanged: like two children fighting over dominoes. "Don't go," she advised Lianna.

"If I do not, he will tell Mama that I went down to the conservatory last night with Sir John. Aubery has said quite disagreeable things to me about it, and really, it *was* quite innocent," she added in a voice of injured virtue. "Sir John wished to see the miniature orange trees that Mama had sent to her from the Indies."

"In the dark," Aubery said with a sardonic curl of his lips.

Lianna turned away from him with a sniff, as if she would not deign to answer his absurd implication. "Why don't you come with us, Pip?" she suggested. "Lady Wright would like that even better, I think, and then I should not have to sit bored to flinders while Aubery makes calf eyes at that silly widgeon Lydia Wright."

Aubery was about to take umbrage at this disparagement of his beloved. But Philippa quickly forestalled him. "I thank you, but no. I have a book to return to the lending library and some threads to match for the chair cover I am making. I don't fancy playing mediator, in any case," she added as she turned to go into the breakfast room.

As soon as she had eaten, she changed for the street and took the light town carriage to the lending library. Changing her book took a matter of minutes, but she paused amid the rows of neatly arranged books to see what new titles were being offered. She was so engrossed in this that she did not pay the least attention when someone else entered her aisle. "I hope you have found something to please you," said a soft voice at her elbow, and she turned to see Francis standing beside her.

He was not looking terribly well for his indulgent evening. His eyes were heavy and his sandy hair had a limp quality; even the usual immaculate arrangement of his neckcloth was less than perfect this morning. His manner seemed mildly aggrieved, but when he spoke, his tone was more sheepish than bellicose. "I've come to beg your pardon, Pip, in more ways than one. I should not have said those things last night. Charlotte told me you did not wish your inheritance to be known just yet, but I was castaway and thought myself a clever fellow for being the first with the news."

"Did you also think yourself clever when you implied to anyone who would listen that my chief attraction was my purse?"

"Did I do that?" He groaned. Another patron entered the row of books across from them, bringing their tête-à-tête to an end. "We can't talk here," he said.

"I am not sure that I wish to speak with you, Francis," Philippa said, and realized that it was true. Confronting him, she found she was angrier and more exacerbated than she had supposed.

"Please," he said. It was not begging, nor was it a command such as Crispin would have given; it was the simple request of a reasonable man, and as such, it touched her more than pleading could have done.

"My aunt's carriage awaits me," she said. "We can speak as we drive home."

He agreed and they left the library at once. Francis assisted her into the town carriage and gave the instructions to the coachman, which Philippa suspected included a drive through the park before they headed for Carnavon House. She did not object; having made up her mind to do so, she was now anxious to hear him. The thought occurred, making her heart beat a little faster, that the hour she had waited and schemed for had come. Francis might at last bare his heart to her and declare himself openly.

"Dash it, Pip," he said at once, "we can't go on like this. I don't know what happened to turn you from me to Cris. It was a dreadful blow when you told me you were betrothed to him, but I swore I wouldn't wear my heart on my sleeve. I pledged to myself that I would never speak of it if you did not do so first, but you have not.

"Whatever you may say," he went on unhappily, "I can't believe you've tumbled out of love with me and into love with Cris all but overnight. I know I behaved very badly last night, but it was seeing you with Cris and knowing that you are his now. It was more than I could reasonably bear."

The sincerity of his tone was not to be denied. Philippa wondered why she was not more affected by it, and supposed that she was still too angry with him for the hurt he had dealt her. Certainly there was none of the joy of triumph she had expected would be her dominant emotions. "So you thought that you would respond in kind and behave unreasonably," she said levelly.

"I deserve that, I know," he said quietly.

"You do, and more," she agreed. "I did not intend

to tell you this, for I did not wish you to think it had anything to do with my decision to marry Crispin, but I know full well that while you made love to me, convincing me that it was best if we kept our attachment quiet until you bettered your position in the world, you made love to Lia as well. She showed me the letter that you sent to her from Leicester asking her to meet you in Lady MacReath's garden. Clandestine affairs appear to be your forte."

He winced a little at this last. "What excuse can I give you, Pip? How can I ask you to forgive me? I was a fool; it was you that I cared for, I know that now. Lia is a lovely child, but we should never suit."

"Did you think her portion would suit you?"

"I fear it did influence me," he said in a low, shamed manner.

Philippa pursed her lips. "This is a bit sudden, is it not, Francis? Last night you learn of my dowry and today you come to ask me to forgive you and tell me that you are still in love with me. It is called cream-pot love, I believe."

"No," Francis said quite forcefully, taking her hands in his. "Pip, whatever you may believe, the only thing I am guilty of is poor timing. I was damn near devastated that you should prefer Cris to me. At first I told myself that if you were that fickle he was welcome to you, but it was only to mask my true feelings. By the end of that week I wanted to throw myself at your feet, beg you to be mine again, but my damnable pride wouldn't let me."

"Very eloquent," Philippa interjected, but she could not but be affected by his words. They were so exactly what she had wished him to say.

"Pip, please don't tell me I haven't any hope," he implored. "The reason I went to Horely to that dashed cockfight was that I couldn't bear to see you beside

Cris accepting the congratulations of all our friends. Lord, every time I saw Cris I wanted to plant him a facer." He smiled suddenly and added self-deprecatingly, "If I could, which I doubt. He spars with Jackson himself." His smile faded. "The reason I came back last night was that I knew I couldn't just let it happen. I had to see you, talk to you, beg you to come back to me."

"And you thought my betrothal ball the place for this?" she asked, incredulous.

He shook his head and raised his fingers briefly to his lips. "No. I returned late in the afternoon. I meant to see you before the ball, but I went to Boodle's first. I didn't realize until I was here how difficult it would be for me to open my heart to you and bear my pride, and I thought that perhaps a little fortification would help." He smiled wryly. "I should have known better. I never have had a head for spirits; Crispin was the one to receive our father's hard head. I had a few glasses of wine and then switched to brandy after dinner. It was a mistake."

"It was," she agreed without warmth.

"I don't deserve you, Pip, I know that," he said, his eyes effectively conveying his wretchedness. "But I love you and I want you and you can consign your inheritance to the nearest orphanage for all I care. I only wish with all my heart that I had come to you the moment I arrived in town. Then I would not have known of your cursed fortune and I might now have hope." He paused, clearly waiting for her to respond, but she did not. "Say that you don't really love Cris," he begged. "Give me that at least."

Philippa withdrew her hand from his, but she gave him what he wanted. "I am not in love with Crispin," she said quietly, not looking at Francis. "But there is feeling between us," she added, and realized that it was true. There was physical attraction if nothing else.

"That is no way to plight your troth, Pip. Not when there could be love between us."

"Are you asking me to jilt Crispin and marry you, Francis?"

"With all my heart," he said fervently.

This was it: the words she had wanted to hear above all others for the last five years. But Philippa felt curiously unmoved; assent to his plea did not rush to her lips. Perhaps it was a remnant of her displeasure with Francis, or only anticlimax, but she knew she did not want to say yes, at least not just yet. She still believed that she wished to marry Francis, and did not know what was making her capricious.

"I am not sure that I can," she heard herself say doubtfully.

"Of course you can," Francis assured her. "You need only tell him that you are in love with me and he'll release you from your promise, I am certain of it."

"You misunderstand, Francis," she said levelly. "I am not sure that I wish to marry you now."

His jaw dropped and his brow creased. "You don't love Cris, you've said so."

"But I have not said that I still love you."

He was silent for a moment and then said, "Cris will make you a damnable husband. You can only hope that he doesn't game away the whole of your inheritance and leave you alone at nights to darn your own petticoats."

Philippa smiled. "And you would not use my fortune to your purposes?"

"I would use it to assure our future."

"*Our* future, Francis?"

"You accuse me of an interest in your fortune, but I would wager the equal of it that Cris had no more intention than I of marrying a portionless woman,"

Francis said with asperity. "I at least love you, you know that. He thinks of nothing but your purse."

"There was no fortune that he knew of when he asked me to marry him."

"No?" Francis' smile was condescending.

"I only learned of my cousin's death and the legacy the day before yesterday," she said. "You must know that."

"I don't know how Cris knew before you, but I am certain that he did," Francis insisted. "He as good as told me so just after you told me of the betrothal."

Philippa was aware of an uncomfortable inward feeling. "I don't believe that," she said deliberately. "Damning Cris won't make me think better of you."

"It's no lie. We spoke of your having so little portion and he said that he suspected that you would prove to be a greater prize than we thought."

There was that in the phrasing of those words that was unmistakably Crispin. The discomfort within her grew, though she did not know why. "That means nothing. Likely it was just a passing remark."

"I don't think so," Francis replied, and the confidence in his voice was damnably convincing. "Don't believe me if you like," he advised her. "Ask Cris what he meant when he said it. I'll give him this, he's devilish honest."

"Which is more than you are," Philippa said, her anger returning in full measure. "You would have betrayed me with my own cousin."

Having taken a circuitous route, the carriage at last pulled up before Carnavon House. There was no chance for Francis to answer this, for a footman, with great efficiency, had already come out of the house to let down the carriage steps and open the door.

Philippa exited the carriage without so much as looking at him again. Picking up her book, which she had left forgotten on the seat, he followed her into the house. He took hold of her arm as he caught up with her at the bottom of the staircase. "Pip—" he began, but she cut him off.

"There is really nothing else to say, Francis," she said coolly. "Unless you wish for a formal reply to your offer. I thank you for the honor you do me, but I must refuse."

She did not wait to hear his response to this, but turned and continued up the stairs, thus missing the furious expression that crossed his pleasant features and the violent manner in which he threw down her book on the checked marble floor. The astonished butler and his underling watched, mouths agape, as Lord Francis turned abruptly and left the house again. Johnson retrieved the abused book thoughtfully and advised the footman to find occupation other than gawking at his betters.

Philippa spent much of the remainder of the morning reviewing her relationship with Francis and trying to understand her feelings toward him now. She had had other suitors to her hand besides Francis, but these had found scant encouragement. Philippa had never given any other man the least consideration, always believing and expecting to marry Francis. How could it be then that when he finally said the words she thought she longed to hear, she had rejected him quite out of hand. It was true that Francis had hurt and infuriated her, but she found it hard to believe that her love for him, so long nurtured, had so easily died.

It was equally hard to believe that all of her dreams and desires had been turned upside down in so short a space of time. Little more than a fortnight ago she had felt secure in her life and the future she hoped for; now she did not seem to know what she wanted, or even

why she felt the way she did. Was she falling out of
love with Francis or was she just going through the
painful adjustment of seeing him as a real man
complete with flaws instead of the perfect lover she
had imagined him to be?

Neither was it easy for her to admit that her judgment of Crispin had been formed so completely by
what Francis had told her of him. She had believed all
that Francis had said, never thinking that his own
judgment might be colored by his envy of his brother.
But she realized now that this was what had happened. Crispin was certainly no pattern card of virtue
any more than Francis, but he did not display the
dissolute character that Francis gave him.

Yet Philippa did not think it was Francis' vituperation against Crispin, nor even his attentions to Lianna,
that had changed her heart. She believed the sticking
point was that she could not believe that learning of
her inheritance last night had played no part in his
declaration this morning.

She dismissed as spite Francis' contention that
Crispin had in any way known of her inheritance or
guessed at the future. Even if he had, Crispin had not
offered for her willingly and she could not believe that
the fantastic set of coincidences that had led to her
abduction and their subsequent betrothal had been
contrived.

But such was the doubting tenor of Philippa's mind
that she could not quite allow Francis' accusation to
be. She did not know what difference it made to her,
since she still had no intention of marrying Crispin.
She supposed she ought to start thinking at once of a
reasonable way to end their betrothal, since it had
served its purpose, but she could not seem to put her
mind to the task. Crispin was out most of the day, but

when she heard him return, she followed him to his dressing room, determined at least to put the doubts that Francis had planted to rest.

The door was opened by Crispin himself, but his manservant, Collins, was already in the room, which made Philippa feel a bit awkward. She sent a speaking glance in his direction and Crispin obediently turned and dismissed the valet. But he went to his dressing table and began to remove his neckcloth, for the dinner hour was nearly upon them. He noted Philippa's unsmiling countenance and air of purpose. "What is it now, my dear Pip?" he said with an air of resignation. "Have you come to throw my betrothal ring at my feet again?"

"No, or at least not yet. It is something else." Philippa followed him across the room.

He looked up at her through the mirror over the dressing table. A faint smile touched his lips. "You greatly relieve me. Yet I fancy you still regard me as if I were an insect turned up under a leaf in your salad."

A brief smile softened Philippa's expression. "You are absurd," she said mechanically and quickly added, "I have a question that I must ask you." He indicated that she should go on and she took a breath and said, "Did you tell Francis that you suspected my portion was worth more than was apparent?"

She saw by his expression that she had for once successfully caught him off guard. "It surprises me that you would swallow any of the poison he was spreading last night."

His surprise was brief and his expression was now guarded, but Philippa watched him carefully for any betraying emotion. "It isn't that. I told him this morning that I did not believe it, but he suggested that I ask you myself if it were so."

"Did he?" Crispin's smile was sardonic. "My brother is not slow to use what he can to his advantage."

"He also said he did not think you would lie to me. Will you, Cris?"

"I must remember to thank him for that encomium." Crispin sighed. "I can see that parson's mousetrap will be tight indeed. The night that I met you in the gardens of MacReath House, you will recall, I had no notion that it was you I was abucting, and I can assure you I was as astonished and dismayed as you were yourself when I discovered my mistake. If you wish for absolutely plain speaking, until I realized that I had unwittingly compromised you and that in our separate ways we could both face ruin for that night's work, I never had the least notion of asking you to be my wife, fortune or no."

But Philippa could be tenacious and she felt he had evaded a direct answer to her question. "Then you had no knowledge of my inheritance on that night?"

He gave an exasperated little sigh. "Haven't I just said so?"

"Not really."

Their eyes locked for a long moment in the oval glass and then he sighed again in quite a different way. "Damn Francis," he said softly. "He is quite right, I won't lie to you about this. I didn't know the extent of your inheritance, or the terms of it, but I did know of Lord Tamary's death and the fact that you were to receive some sort of legacy from him."

Philippa sat down in the nearest chair assailed with a disappointment that she understood no better than her reason for rejecting Francis this morning. She did not know why it should matter to her, but it did, very much so. She knew she was hurt by his admission; perhaps it was the fear that no man sought her for herself alone. "How could you know?" she asked tonelessly. "Not even I knew until the day before yesterday."

He was silent for a time, as if weighing his words. "I received a letter from my solicitor in Edinburgh concerning a bit of property there that I have been trying to sell. He is not the same man employed by your uncle, but is of the same firm, and I fear he was indiscreet."

"You never said a word to me," Philippa said accusingly.

"It was none of my affair."

"You did not even think I might wish to know of my cousin's passing?"

"You and Aubery both have said often enough how little regard there was there on either side, and my man told me that it was deliberately not being announced until after the burial by a direct provision in the will."

"And you promptly forgot the matter entirely," Philippa suggested sarcastically.

"Hardly," he admitted with a faint smile. "I thought it would be an impertinence for me to involve myself in your concerns. You would learn of it soon enough, and the delay would in no way change the legacy."

Philippa picked up a pearl-inlaid snuffbox that lay on the dressing table and turned it over slowly as if examining it in detail. "Last night," she said suddenly, "were you discussing horses with Lady Vernay?" Only when she had completed her question did she look up at him for his reaction.

He laughed with surprise. "Curiously enough, I was. Letty is an old friend, but we have never been lovers. Why?"

"It might be expected that I would be interested in

knowing that," she said acerbically, putting down the snuffbox and looking away from him again.

"Why?" he repeated. "You never miss an opportunity to inform me how little you care for me or wish to be my wife."

She didn't answer. She stood and began walking about the room, pausing occasionally to examine some item on a table or bureau top. "Did you plan that meeting in the garden and intend to compromise me so that I would have to marry you?"

"I should be flattered for your opinion of my cleverness, but I must confess the truth. I did not." He turned on the stool in front of the dressing table and looked at her.

She, too, turned and faced him. "I never had the least intention of going through with the wedding," she said with sudden resolution. "I only agreed because you were being so disagreeable and because I hoped that it would make Francis realize, when he thought he had lost me, just how much he wanted me."

"Did it?" he asked without expression.

"Yes."

"I see. Do you love Francis so very much?"

"I thought I did."

"Thought?"

"He asked me to marry him this morning. I refused him."

"Very wise of you, my dear. You may recall that you are already, ah, encumbered."

"I hoped you would release me when I told you the truth."

"You have great faith in my understanding nature," he said dryly. He sighed. "Do you still wish me to release me from your promise?"

Philippa was surprised by this. "I—I suppose that I

do. That is, we certainly should not suit. It would be better, I think, to face a bit of scandal than to find ourselves tied to each other for life."

"I don't agree," he said, and rose and went over to where she stood near the mantel. "There are times when I think we should suit very well. When he isn't intriguing—a failing common to politicians, I fear—Francis is a dull sort of fellow. You, my dear, Philippa, are a woman of honor and spirit. You deserve better."

"Such as you?" Philippa asked archly.

He threw back his head and laughed. "Yes." He sobered again. "So little regard had I for your fortune, I wanted this betrothal no more than you did. I cursed you heartily for bringing me to heel, however unintentionally. I am not quite sure what has effected the change in me, but, my dear Philippa, I have come to think you are the loveliest, most fascinating woman I have ever known. You shoot at me with my own pistol, you box my ears when I try to make love to you, and yet I find that it is no longer that I *must* marry you, it is with all my heart what I wish to do. I have fallen in love with you, fair charmer."

Philippa was nothing short of stunned, and there was another, less readily defined emotion. She could scarcely believe what she had heard; her heartbeat, which was so often erratic in his presence, began to pound so rapidly and loudly that she thought for certain he must hear it. This time she could not readily convince herself that it was caused by anger or outrage. Dear Lord, what was happening to her? She could not credit that she had tumbled out of love with Francis and into love with his brother.

She was silent for so long that Crispin took it for encouragement and, leaning forward, kissed her lightly. Pleased with the response he found there, he enfolded her in his arms and repeated the action with renewed vigor. He was a little surprised, then, to be pushed away with a sudden decisiveness. "What is it, Pip?" he asked gently. "You are not indifferent to me. I would wager my life on it."

"No. I don't think I am," she admitted. And then she said in a quieter way, "But I don't think that it makes me wish to marry you."

There had been a sort of boyish exuberance in his features, and this now dissipated. "Then it is Francis," he said flatly.

"I don't know what it is," Philippa replied with perfect truth. "I cannot be in love with Francis one day and you the next," she said with some vehemence, as though she wished to convince herself of this. "It would be unpardonably stupid."

"Stupid?"

"Do you suppose that you need only tell me you love me and I shall forget that you knew of my inheritance before we were betrothed and said nothing of it to me?" she said, though she found it curiously painful to do so. "Francis, too, attempted to convince me that he had no thought for my fortune. I think there is more in common between you than I had supposed."

His features set and he regarded her in a way that was hard to read. "You know damn well I've never been hanging out for a rich wife. I haven't a grand fortune to go with my title, but I'm no pauper. I don't give a damn for your inheritance."

This was so nearly what Francis had said to her that instead of finding his words reassuring, she only feared that it was exactly what a fortune-hunter would say to set his victim at ease. "Perhaps you wish me to give it away?" she asked scathingly.

"Of course not," he replied coldly. "That *would* be

stupid. Nor would I suggest that we tie it up in our progeny. I expect that I shall like having a rich wife well enough."

His honesty was disarming, and Philippa felt more confused than ever. Again his manner turned gentle; the abrupt, passionate way his moods could change was not unattractive and she could not help herself responding to him once again as he took both her hands in his. "Philippa, I know that I told you that I hadn't any desire to marry any woman, but I was wrong and I knew it even as I said it. I knew that I loved you, but I needed to know better what there was yet between you and Francis, and then there *was* your damnable inheritance." He raised one of her hands to his lips and kissed her fingertips. "It had already occurred to me that if I were to suddenly begin making love to you now in earnest, you might suspect my motives, which you obviously do." Again the disarmingly rueful smile. "But subtlety, I fear, is not my style. Perhaps I simply love you too much to dissemble any longer."

No wonder he was a successful rake, she thought. Her senses and mind were reeling. She wanted to believe him so badly that it was nearly a physical thing. I can't love this man, she told herself firmly, but she knew that she did. She knew he was going to kiss her again and she would not have prevented him, but at that moment the door from the hall opened and Aubery barged into the room.

"The devil," he exclaimed as he took in the scene before him. "Damme, if this don't beat all. Oil and water trying to mix."

"Your opinions are not solicited, cub," Crispin said coolly. "And your presence is decidedly *de trop.*"

But the moment had passed and Philippa had already withdrawn from the spell his words and nearness had created. "I had better dress or I shall be late for dinner," she said in a voice that was amazingly commonplace. She fled the room, not knowing whether Crispin would tender any explanation to her brother and not particularly caring.

8

Lady Carnavon, her daughter, and her niece, were to attend the opera that evening with a party of friends and planned to go on from there to an assembly at Lady Ponsonby's. Philippa thought of crying off with an invented headache, but she suspected that Crispin would arrange his own plans so that he would remain at home and have the chance to speak with her again. She wanted some time to herself before they resumed their broken discussion. She believed she was in love with him, but she did not understand how that could be, and neither was she sure that she could trust him.

The opera, *Le Nozze di Figaro*, was a favorite of Philippa's, but so lost was she in her own cogitations that she scarcely heard it. During the interval she replied mechanically to the comments of friends who visited their box, and by the time the opera had ended, she knew she could not go on to the assembly pretending that there was nothing at all in her mind but the pursuit of the evening's pleasures.

Lady Carnavon was naturally concerned when Philippa begged to be allowed to return to Grosvenor Square, but she acquiesced readily enough and went along with her niece's insistence that she and Lianna go on to the assembly without her. The dowager was not the most perceptive of women, but she was clever enough to realize that something was going forward in her house and that it somehow revolved about her niece and her two stepsons.

Francis had been strangely glum and snappish all day, and his drunken behavior the night before had been unusual enough to make her wonder. Crispin did not appear on the surface to be any other than he usually was, but Lady Carnavon had noticed him watching both Francis and Philippa in a speculative manner. It made her watch them, too, and matching this to some of the odd comments Philippa had made concerning her betrothal, she began to have some inkling of the truth.

They met Aubery at the Ponsonbys' and he was utterly lacking in his usual exuberance, which Lianna managed to discover was due to the fact that he had heard that Miss Wright—the drive to Richmond, not withstanding—had at last accepted an offer of marriage from Lord Hobarth and was lost to him forever.

"Perhaps you shall fall into a decline and let your health go to ruin," Lianna suggested without much sympathy. "That would show her how heartless she was."

"Men don't go into declines," Aubery said severely, momentarily annoyed out of his languishing attitude.

"I don't see why not," Lianna insisted. "If a woman may have her heart broken, why cannot a man?"

"It is probably all pose," Aubery said petulantly. "Your sex hasn't any heart to break. Even Pip, whom I've always thought of as the most constant woman I know, has proved herself no better than the rest of her sex."

Lady Carnavon overheard this comment, but could

not persuade Aubery to elaborate on it; he would only animadvert of the fickleness of females in general and of Miss Wright in particular. But the dowager was not put off by his evasion and determined to get to the bottom of the matter. Accordingly she sought out her niece the moment they returned and found her not prostate on her bed as she had claimed she would be, but sitting in a chair in her sitting room reading a favorite novel.

Lady Carnavon bent over her niece's chair and kissed her lightly on the forehead. "I am glad the headache has left you, my love, but you did miss a delightful assembly. Caro Lamb was there, of course, and raving about the poet fellow, Lord Byron, who is one of the mad Gordons, I believe. I cannot say that *Childe Harold* was really to my taste, but one reads such things of course to be *au courant.*" She chatted on in this vein for several minutes longer, and though Philippa responded with the proper words in the proper places, it was obvious that her usual interest in the adventures and foibles of her friends and acquaintances was no better than tepid at best.

Lady Carnavon broke off in the middle of a story about the Duke of Gloucester, and Philippa scarcely seemed to notice. "I fear something quite other than a headache is troubling you tonight, my dear, is it not?"

Philippa took her finger out of her book and closed it with finality. She had not thought to look for a confidante, but she needed someone to convince her that it would not be a complete mistake to marry a man who was a self-confessed rake, who was arrogant, who had deceived her, and who might well be more in love with her new fat purse than with her. She acknowledged that all was not well with her. "I don't know why I am being so stupid. I don't seem to know what I think, or feel, or . . . or anything."

Lady Carnavon's brows rose. This was out of character for her niece, who always seemed to know exactly what it was she wanted. "Why don't you tell me about it, love?" she said coaxingly. "You know you may trust me to say nothing to anyone, including your Uncle Henry, if you do not wish it known."

Philippa gave her tacit consent to this by leaving her chair to share a sofa with her aunt. "Is it possible to fall out of love with one man and fall into love with another in the space of a day?" she asked with a doleful smile.

Lady Carnavon returned the smile, congratulating herself for having guessed so near the truth. "I don't think so, my love. I think that one falls out of love and into it again at a more gradual pace, but it is the realization of the change in one's feelings that comes all at once."

Philippa had for so long kept her feelings for Francis to herself that she found it a little difficult to share them now. Starting a bit haltingly, she told her aunt of her long-standing attachment to Francis, the true reason she had allowed herself to become betrothed to Crispin, and her own inability to understand how the desired result of this had proven so unsatisfactory.

"I had no notion I was so obtuse," the dowager exclaimed when she was done. "I might have understood if you had formed such a strong attachment for Crispin, for young girls are forever imagining themselves in love with dashing men of the town. But neither you nor Francis ever appeared to give each other any special notice."

Philippa managed a short laugh. "I prided myself on my cleverness at keeping everyone from suspecting. I suppose it was as much a game to me as it was a romance. It seems almost foolish to me now that I agreed so readily to wait until Francis had established himself before so much as acknowledging our love."

"And when would that have been?" Lady Carnavon asked tartly. "For every Pitt who is a success in politics before thirty, there are fifty men who never see success before they are in their dotage."

"I thought I loved him," Philippa said simply. "I wanted to believe him. But when he finally declared himself, I felt nothing."

Lady Carnavon patted her niece's hand. "Which was quite his own fault. He could not suppose that you would wait on his time indefinitely. You are a lovely young woman, Pip, there was bound to be someone else to attract you. You suppose it is Carnavon." She saw Philippa's startled expression and said, "Who else would it be? And a very good thing, too, if you are going to be his wife."

Philippa sighed. "I never intended to be his wife, and yet now he claims that he loves me and I am wretched because I cannot convince myself that this is true, or at least disinterested with regard to my inheritance. How can I have been so sure of myself two days ago and now so unsure of how I should go on?"

The dowager had no set answer for this but neither had Philippa expected that she would. It was enough that she had been able to speak her fears and uncertainties aloud. It helped her common sense reassert itself over her emotions and she realized that it was not imperative that she know her mind and heart at once.

Lady Carnavon's heart went out to Philippa, who she knew would feel her confusion the worse for not being a romantic miss like her own daughter, who seemed to tumble in and out of love almost as frequently as she changed gowns. If the circumstances were different, she would have preferred to see Philippa married to a man with a less volatile nature than her elder stepson possessed, but she was forced to admit that late events had proven Crispin less erratic than his brother, whom she had always regarded as the steadier of the two.

It was not in Philippa's nature to go about in low spirits, but Lady Carnavon thought she noticed a bit less sparkle about her niece than was usual. It scarcely helped that her mourning for her uncle forced her to sit among the chaperones and dowds at any event that contained dancing or lively activity. The dowager thought that quite enough to cast down anyone's spirits even if there were nothing else to trouble them.

The Carnavon estate might not have constituted a great fortune, but the jewels that were a part of it were really quite splendid. When the dowager had married Crispin's father, she had enjoyed the use of the collection, several pieces of which were exquisitely wrought and quite well known. But Charlotte Carnavon did not have any particular attachment for jewels, and beyond using them as accessories to complement her gowns, she seldom gave them much thought. She would find it no hardship at all to turn the Carnavon jewels over to her niece when Philippa became the new Lady Carnavon.

Thinking that perhaps it might cheer Philippa to have a sapphire earring-and-pendant set she had always particularly admired presented to her for use even before the wedding, Lady Carnavon removed from the bottom of her wardrobe the large leather case that held most of the Carnavon collection. She pushed the bottles of scent and cosmetics to the back of her dressing table and with some difficulty—for it was quite heavy—she placed the case on top of the dressing table, unlocked it, and began to pull out the drawers to find the set she had in mind to give to Philippa.

It nestled in its usual place in the second drawer but

Lady Carnavon scarcely noticed it. Her dresser, coming into the room at that moment, found her staring openmouthed at the open, and quite empty, top drawer of the case, and when the maid asked in a tentative way if something was amiss, her mistress turned wide eyes on her and said in a stunned voice, "The Carnavon diamonds!"

The dresser, a very superior personage known as Walker, replied with only a slightly confused sounding "Yes, my lady?" But then she looked down at the empty drawer and began to understand. "You haven't taken the diamonds out of the case yourself, my lady?"

Lady Carnavon shook her head unhappily. "And I don't suppose you have sent them to Rundell and Bridge to be cleaned."

The maid indicated that she had not, and a look of apprehension spread over her features, for it was her duty to look after all of her ladyship's things, including the Carnavon jewels. If anything were missing or out of order, it would reflect badly on her. The necklace, known throughout the *ton* as the Carnavon diamonds, dated from the time of Queen Anne and was famed not only for its original beauty, but for the fortune it was said to be worth. If it were mislaid, it would be the ruin of her career as an upper servant; if proved to be stolen, it would go far, far worse for the luckless dresser unless the thief were discovered and she cleared of all complicity.

But the look that her mistress bent on her was not the least accusatory, only puzzled and anxious. "The last time I wore them was at my niece's betrothal ball," she said. She pulled out the remaining drawers and rummaged through them as if she might move aside an earring and discover the large, many-faceted necklace beneath it. She then removed the top drawer altogether and placed her hand in the empty slot. "I am certain that we put them away that night before I went to bed. I distinctly remember . . ." She broke off suddenly and only went on again at the prompting of her servant. "Well, perhaps I am mistaken," she said as she quickly returned the top drawer to the case and shut it firmly. She put down the lid of the case and turned the key in the lock. "I suppose I might have thrown them into some drawer, meaning it only to be overnight."

"Oh, no, my lady," Walker assured her. A bit put out at the assumption that she would be so derelict in her duties to allow such a thing. "I am sure that they were placed safely in the case that night."

"Then I may have had them out again and mislaid them," Lady Carnavon said a bit testily. "If I have a minute to myself, no doubt it will come to me what I have done with them."

Protesting all the way that she would be happy to help her ladyship locate the jewels, Walker was pushed firmly to the door by her mistress, who adjured her not to mention to anyone that the diamonds were missing until it was quite certain that they were not simply mislaid. When the door was shut firmly against intrusion, Lady Carnavon returned to her dressing table and again unlocked the case. Pulling out the top drawer, she reached into the space where the drawer had been again, and removed an odd-shaped opal that was neither quite round nor precisely oval. She stared at it for several moments, turning it over in her fingers. It was no more than a single stone, but she did not doubt its ownership. She had seen this unusual-shaped stone too many times in the ring that her elder stepson so often wore. She dropped onto the nearest chair and covered her mouth is dismay.

"You are a foolish old woman, Charlotte," she told herself aloud, but the thought would not be banished.

In her mind she could remember Crispin's dry comment at the ball on the state of his finances and the solution he had suggested. He had only been joking when he had said it, she was sure, but perhaps the idea had been born for him then and he had acted upon it after all.

She despised herself for thinking it, but if he had not removed the diamonds from her jewel case, then how had the opal come to be there? With all of her might she tried to recall the last time she had seen him wearing the ring. But the ring was so much a part of his usual adornment that it proved impossible. She supposed that she took it for granted that he wore it even when he did not.

Technically, since the death of his father, the diamonds had belonged to Crispin, but they were part of the entailed estate and not his to the extent that he was free to dispose of them as he wished. Lady Carnavon had never known Crispin to be irresponsible on any matter concerning the welfare of the estate before, but she supposed it was possible that Crispin had convinced himself that the diamonds were his even if it was more of a trust than an actual ownership. He would know that she would never countenance his taking the diamonds. If he had taken the diamonds without telling her, it was likely that he was having a glass copy made to keep it from being known. It was just his misfortune that she had opened the top drawer by mistake when looking for the pendant, and that he had not had the time or the opportunity to put the glass necklace in place.

She did not want to think ill of her stepson. Though she had perhaps at times favored Francis for his more steady ways, she thoroughly liked Crispin, for she had always found him good-natured, generous, and never underhanded. It was hard to believe that he had stooped to so low an act.

Perhaps the circumstances he found himself in had brought him to this. If Crispin were trying to convince Philippa that he cared not at all for her fortune, it would be a difficult thing for him to have to enter the marriage with gaming debts. Of course, she did not really know the extent of his indebtedness, or if he lacked the means of settling them. She had only his own, half-facetious comment at the betrothal ball to go by, but it had always been her experience that gentlemen tended to downplay such obligations to her sex than otherwise.

Lady Carnavon did not want for practical sense, but she was not at all sure what she should do now. She supposed the easiest thing would be to do nothing at all. If Crispin was having the jewels copied, doubtless in a day or two the "diamonds" would return to their usual place in the leather case; he would not be foolish or arrogant enough to simply take the diamonds and leave their absence to speculation. But she could not like this. She felt it was nothing short of complicity and nearly as dishonest as if she had taken the diamonds herself.

She was so caught up in her thoughts and the indecision they caused that when she heard the faint tap at her door, she bid whoever knocked enter without realizing that the last thing she wished for at this moment was company. She became aware of what she had done almost as soon as the word was out of her mouth and she jumped up and said, "No, don't come in," at exactly the same moment that Philippa came into the room.

Philippa's smile was a bit uncertain. "Why, what is it, Aunt Charlotte? Do I disturb you?"

"No—that is, yes. I am quite busy just now." As she spoke, she rose and moved the few steps to stand in front of her dressing table to hide as best she could the leather case that stood open upon it. Philippa was the last person she wished to have know of her suspicions.

But her movements were quick and unnatural, and instead of deflecting Philippa's attention, they increased it. "What are you doing, Aunt?" she asked. "Are you going through your jewels? I'll help you if you like and in any case it is exactly what I wished to see you about."

"About what?" Lady Carnavon said more sharply than she intended.

Philippa's brows knit. "Whatever is the matter with you, Aunt? Is there something amiss?"

"No. What should be?" Lady Carnavon said with an attempted lightness that would have fooled no one. In a nervous gesture she made to pat an escaping tendril of hair into place, quite forgetting that she held the opal in her hand, and when she opened her fingers, it dropped to the floor, making no noise on the Turkey carpet, but taking a little hop that carried across the room to land almost at Philippa's feet. Lady Carnavon's eyes rounded with horror and she had the wild thought of scrambling after it, but she recognized the absurdity of this and only stood still, waiting to see what Philippa would make of it.

Philippa examined the small stone. "Why, this is from Cris' ring, surely? Has he given you the ring to have it repaired?" Lady Carnavon nearly sagged with relief at having this excuse handed to her and she replied quickly that that was it precisely. "Oh, I do hope that you are sending out the ruby earrings to be cleaned," Philippa continued as she handed the opal back to her aunt. "I came to ask you to lend them to me tonight. I thought a bit of color would bring my gray silk to life."

"Of course you may have the rubies," Lady Carnavon said a little too quickly. "In a few months they shall be yours, in any case. When you are dressing, I'll send Walker to you with them."

Philippa was genuinely puzzled by her aunt's behavior, but if the older woman did not wish to explain herself, she would not be ill-bred and push the confidence. "There is no need to trouble Walker," she said. "As long as you have the case open, I'll take them now."

It was a reasonable request and Lady Carnavon was hard put to think of an excuse not to comply with it, but she did not want Philippa to see the empty, pulled-out drawer. There was no reason for Philippa to realize that the diamonds were missing, but in her anxious state Lady Carnavon feared exactly that.

Philippa saw the other's obvious indecision and decided to consign breeding to the devil. "Please tell me what is the matter, Aunt Charlotte?" she coaxed gently. "I know there is something troubling you."

"It is the most trifling matter, my dear," the dowager answered a little shortly, annoyed with herself for behaving so stupidly. "Of course you may have the earrings now," she added, and turned around quickly, trying to return the empty drawer to the case before Philippa could see it.

Philippa had stepped closer to the dressing table and had a few view of the case and her aunt's actions. She would have thought nothing of the empty drawer if Lady Carnavon had had the sense not to call her attention to it. As it was, she realized at once that that was where the Carnavon diamonds were usually kept and that the necklace was not now in place. Even so she did not at once realize the import of this absence. "Never say you have mislaid the Carnavon diamonds, Aunt Charlotte," she said with a laugh, intending it as a bit of quizzing only.

But these words were the last straw for the flustered marchioness. She caught her breath and cast her niece a look so stricken that Philippa summed up the situation at once. "Oh, Aunt, it is not that?" she said.

"No, at least not precisely." Lady Carnavon sounded close to tears.

Philippa closed the jewel case and, putting her arm around her aunt, drew her to the chaise longue near the fire. "Are you quite sure of it?" she asked gently. "It is likely that you have simply put them in safe-keeping in another place. Was my betrothal ball the last time you wore them?"

"Yes, I think so." The older woman sighed. "No, it is no use. I am a wretched liar and I won't have you thinking me so shatterbrained that I would forget what I had done with a necklace that is worth a king's ransom. It is missing and I scarcely know what to think."

Philippa hated to say it, but knew that she must. "Is it possible that it has been stolen? Is there anything else missing?"

The dowager shook her head. "Only the diamonds." She turned misery-laden eyes on her niece. "I don't know what else it can be."

"Oh, dear, I wish it weren't so, and not just because a valuable necklace is gone. The only people with easy access to your room would be one of the servants and it will be a wretched business interviewing each and having the pall of suspicion fall over the entire household."

"No." Lady Carnavon's reply was suprisingly vehement. "I am certain it could not be one of the servants. Nearly all of them have been with the Glennon family, one way or another, all of their lives."

"But if you are sure you have not misplaced them and you cannot blame the servants, what solution can you suggest?" Philippa asked logically. "I cannot believe that a burglar had got into the house with no one knowing of it, and surely a professional thief would not stop at taking the diamonds when there were so many other valuable jewels in the case as well. If you had them after the betrothal ball, we at least shall be spared having to suspect any of our friends or acquaintances, for we have not entertained since."

Philippa paused as a sudden thought occurred to her. "Surely you keep the case locked. Was the lock forced in any way? Where do you keep the key?"

"On a chain about my neck," the dowager replied. "I have kept it there since my marriage to Carnavon."

"Is it the only key?"

"No, Crispin has another," Lady Carnavon replied without realizing what she said until the words were out.

But Philippa did not pick up on it. "But I suppose you have left the key with your dresser at times."

"Walker would never steal from me, or even be careless with the key," Lady Carnavon said adamantly.

Philippa sighed. "Yet the diamonds are missing. There is really no one else in the house but the family." Lady Carnavon said nothing and Philippa found her silence more telling than if she had protected. "Aunt Charlotte, you can't think that any one of us would do such a thing." But she scarcely heard the dowager's hasty assurances. She watched her aunt turning the opal over in her fingers in an absent way, remembered her expression when she had dropped the stone, and realized the full import of Lady Carnavon's odd behavior. "You think that Cris has taken them," she said, her voice rising in amazement. "But it is absurd, the Carnavon diamonds are already his. Why would he take them?"

"They are part of the estate," the dowager said dully, not meeting her niece's eyes, "and he hasn't the right to sell them without the consent of his heir."

Philippa felt her throat constrict and her stomach felt as if she had swallowed lead. "Perhaps he is having them . . . reset or some such thing before our wedding," she suggested hopefully.

"Why would he do so without saying anything to me?"

Philippa did not want to believe as her aunt obviously did. "*Did* he give you the opal to have it repaired?" she asked quietly, for she sensed it played some significant part in her aunt's suspicions.

The dowager shook her head sadly. "No, I found it in the jewel case, behind the drawer where the diamonds were kept."

Philippa stood, too agitated to sit. "But why? He told me himself that though the estate does not bring him a great fortune, he finds it to be a competence."

"Gaming debts," the dowager said succinctly.

Philippa had so broken herself from the habit of thinking Crispin as profligate due purely to reputation that she was shocked. "So great that he must needs steal to meet them?"

Lady Carnavon related her theory and it made enough sense that Philippa could not dismiss it out of hand. As she listened and supplied her own mental embellishment based on various things that Crispin had said to her, Philippa's agitation turned to queasiness and then to a curious numbness.

She heard her aunt's tentative ideas about what she

should do next with only half an ear, and when Lady Carnavon suggested that perhaps the best course would be to send for Crispin and ask him plainly if he had taken the diamonds, she agreed without really giving her attention to what she was saying. She had no difficulty agreeing with her aunt that they must say nothing of their discovery to anyone else.

"Especially, we must tell no one that I found Carnavon's opal in the jewel case," she adjured. "If it is at all possible that there is some innocent explanation, we would not wish anyone to form false suspicions against him."

Such as we have ourselves, Philippa thought unhappily. Here was yet another thing to turn her peace upside down. In the time that had passed since she had refused Francis and heard a declaration of love from Crispin, she had spent more time trying to understand her feelings than was her wont. She had successfully avoided situations with Crispin where he could easily renew his lovemaking until she could make up her mind if it was what she truly wished to receive from him.

Crispin seemed to understand this and did not press her. At the least, she was no longer insisting that they find the means of bringing their betrothal to an immediate end. His company was always amusing and never demanding, and Philippa found herself increasingly hungry for it. She had all but made up her mind that she could trust these feelings that she now seemed to have for him, and perhaps even trust him as well. But now all was at sea again.

When she left her aunt, she went down to the small but well-tended formal garden behind the house to walk about in solitude, and once again gave herself up to unprofitable cogitations.

A short while later Crispin found Philippa in a quiet

corner of the garden seated on a stone bench. His approach was quiet and she did not hear him until he was nearly upon her. She was obviously startled to see him and, he thought, not best pleased. His own expression took on a grim aspect. He wasted no time coming to his point. "Do you agree with my stepmother that with all my other sins I am also a thief?" he said with an abruptness that was nearly curt.

"I don't know what I think," she said, rising to face him.

"But you entertain the possibility." It was a statement, not a question. His temper was at full rein and he wanted no qualified answers.

"I don't know," she said unhappily. "It is just that the evidence is so damning. If it were not you, how could the opal have gotten into the jewel case? And you had a key and would not need to force the lock," she added in an imploring tone. "If you had debts, surely you could have confided them to Charlotte. You know how good-hearted she is; she would not even have scolded you for getting in above your head. Or you might have come to me."

His laugh was harsh. "Marry me and be my love, but first hand over your purse? A very pretty figure I should cut. But I should not say so, should I? It is more evidence to damn me." He brought up his left hand and unclenched it, the small, oval opal rested in his palm. He watched the conflicting emotions play in her mobile countenance. There was some doubt there, he thought, but not enough. Believing in his guilt gave both his stepmother and Philippa too easy a solution to ignore. "My gaming debts did not amount to much above a thousand pound. What think you I shall get for the Carnavon diamonds? Not their full worth, of course, I can't sell them openly, which is why I have resorted to theft."

His withering sarcasm had its effect on her. "I don't want to believe it, and either does my aunt."

"But you do."

"I don't know," she said, turning from him.

"Perhaps you believe as my dear stepmama does. She was most understanding; she said that she could quite see how I might mistake my degree of ownership and feel that I had the right to dispose of my own property as I would even if the law says I may not. She is even willing to overlook my fall from grace and advance me the ready to redeem the baubles. If you would like to make a similar offer, I shall weigh the two and accept the best."

"Cris, please don't," she said, her voice sounding tortured.

"Don't what? Expect the trust of the people who know me best? My dear Philippa, if you and Charlotte will have me for a villain, even I begin to think it must be true."

She made no response and after a moment he went on. "Is it obvious only to me that it is no accident that the opal from my ring was found where it was? Call me a thief, if you must, but acquit me for a fool. If the opal came loose from the ring, I would surely notice, if not at once, soon enough to give me cause to hunt it in the one place I would not wish it to be found."

A sudden happier tone occurred to Philippa and she said quickly, "Where is your ring, Cris?" Her eyes went to his hands, eagerly searching for the opal ring, but the finger on which it usually rested was bare. The hope died out of her eyes and posture.

Essaying a sardonic smile, he held up his hand for her closer inspection. "That sets the seal, does it not?" he asked silkily. "Would it do me the least good, I wonder, to tell you that I missed the ring a day or so ago and have been puzzling since what had become of it. Unlike you and Charlotte, I did not immediately suspect my friends of nabbing it for their own gain." His tone was cutting. "I might offer a solution to the mystery, but I am certain you would not like it. I believe I shall keep my counsel until I have more than my suspicions to go on."

This last was spoken with the obvious intent of criticizing her own condemnation of him, and she felt as wretched as he would have had her feel. But still, she could not exonerate him on his own word. If only the opal had not been found where it was, she would have called all else circumstantial. Philippa turned away from him and placed her fingers against her temple, for her head was beginning to throb. "If you mean that it was deliberately placed there, how could that be? Who would do such a thing?"

"It would seem," he said quietly, "that the one thing that does not pass belief is my baseness." He was silent for a long moment. "We seem to have been mistaken in each other," he said at last in a curiously emotionless voice. "But that is presumption, is it not? You never really answered me and I still don't know that you ever did choose me over Francis. I don't suppose it is possible to lose what never was gained.

"Since I choose not to own up to my crime," he said after another pause that Philippa made no attempt to breach, "Charlotte informs me that she would find it untenable to remain longer in my house. She also advises me that she will most generously refrain from publishing my miscreance, even among the family, provided that I have a suitable glass copy made of the necklace so that the theft is not obvious. She further feels it her duty to advise you against continuing with our betrothal and takes it upon herself to concoct some suitable tale to tell the world and maintain your reputation. It would be a greater ruin, I gather, to be married to me."

A part of Philippa wanted to ignore all of her doubts. She suddenly wished with all of her heart that she could reassure him on every point, but she could not. If her newly discovered love for him had not so confused her in the wake of her waning attachment for Francis, it might have been possible for her to ignore the evidence of his own words and of the opal. "I think it might be best to wait the six months of my mourning before making a decision, at least," she said, hedging.

But he would not let it remain so. "So that you may watch to see how much lower I shall stoop? Why not end it now and be done?"

Philippa looked up at him. She was not crying, but her eyes were bright with unshed tears. "Is that what you want?" she said carefully.

"Surely it is best. You could not wish to ally yourself to a thief and a liar." His voice was as steely as his countenance.

Feeling wretched and hollow inside, but believing that it was what he wished, she clung to the tatters of her pride. She favored him with a brief nod, and her expression as barren as his own, she removed the betrothal ring he had given her and held it out to him. He took it with the hand that held the opal, and the two pieces rolled into each other in the palm of his hand.

Their eyes held for a long moment, and then he turned and walked away, out of the garden. She sat again on the bench, feeling as rigid and cold as the stone. She finally walked to the house, her head held high and firm, a dignity maintained for her own sake.

But once she entered the house again through the French doors in the morning room, her control proved its fragility and she was completely overcome with unaccustomed tears. The room was blessedly empty and she wept into her handkerchief as quietly as she could manage with the gulping sobs racking her body.

The door from the hall opened and she wheeled about in horror, fearing it might be Crispin, for she would not for the world have allowed him to see her so devastated on his account. But it was Francis, whose eyes widened with evident concern as he perceived her condition. He was at her side in a trice, embracing her in the most tender way and begging her to confide in him.

Francis was the last person Philippa wished for a confidant at this moment, but she was so wretched that the temptation to share her misery was greater than she could bear. Quite disjointedly, between sniffs and sobs she told him much of what had happened, complying only with the promise that she had given her aunt of saying nothing about the opal found in the jewel case.

"Damn Carnavon," he said fiercely. "Even I did not think he would stoop so low. The evidence seems flimsy enough, though. Are you sure there is not more? It seems unlike Charlotte to convict him so readily on the basis of a chance remark or the fact that he possessed a key to the jewel case."

"It is what she told me," Philippa replied, though she was tempted to tell him the rest to make her own story more credible.

"Perhaps he condemns himself by ending your betrothal," Francis suggested. "If you were to wed him now, he could never hope to keep from the extent of his excesses."

She and Francis were sitting very close on a sofa in the corner of the room and his arm surrounded her, but she made no demur. "My poor little love," he said gently. "You have been used abominably by the Glennons. I can more readily forgive Crispin for stealing the damned necklace than for making you fall in love with him. I admit that I did not treat you as you deserved, but I truly loved you, Pip. He took your heart from me and now he has cast it away. That is unfortunate."

Philippa quite agreed with this assessment and allowed Francis to continue in this vein, recalling the love and the hopes they had once shared and bemoaning all that had come between them.

"Is it too late for us, Pip?" he said all at once. "Let us put all this wretchedness behind us. Allow me to make you mine, and I give you my word you shall never regret it."

"If I were to jilt one brother for the other, it would be the *on-dit* of the Season," she objected, but in her unhappy state, it was not an entirely unpalatable suggestion. It might even serve to convince Crispin that he had never really held her heart, and in her hurt, she desired that very much.

"What of the opinion of the world when our happiness is at stake?" he said earnestly. "We are the ones who shall live with our mistakes. We need only send the announcement ending your betrothal to the papers at once and then go to Doremire for a quiet wedding, perhaps with only Charlotte, Lia, and Aubery if they wish to accompany us. Then we could spend a bit of time at Maverly or visit the property you have just inherited in Scotland. By the time we return to town and set up our own household, a dozen other scandals will have arisen to make us seem commonplace."

Philippa might be bemused by the constant emotional disorder that seemed lately to plague her life, but hardly to the point that she could not persuade herself that she could again love Francis. But if she could not have Crispin, whom she did love, then what did it matter with whom she spent the rest of her life. She was half-convinced that if she managed to come out of all of this with her reputation intact, she would spend the rest of her life plagued by fortune-hunters, so why not have Francis, whom she at least knew and who, she supposed, would make her a decent-enough husband. She certainly had no ambition to remain single and end an aunt for Aubery's brood when he eventually wed. She thought perhaps she would accept Francis' offer for its greatest expediency.

"What will Aunt Charlotte say and Aunt Tess and Uncle Henry?" she said tentatively, for she did not want to accept him too quickly, which might either feed his vanity or make him suspicious of her motive. "They will think I have taken leave of my senses."

"They will think you have come to them," he said firmly, and given the surprise expressed by all of her older relatives when they had learned of her betrothal to Crispin, she supposed it was not without truth. Philippa had herself well in command at last, and she acted with as much cool consideration as the most gazetted of fortune-hunters. She demurred a bit further for effect, but within a quarter-hour, Francis, the vanquished lover, at last knew success.

9

Philippa was very glad of the company of her cousin and aunt on the long carriage drive to Doremire Abbey. Lianna's inconsequential chatter and Lady Carnavon's constant comments on the passing countryside did much to divert her and to keep her mind off the course she was taking. She had accepted Francis' proposal because at the moment it had seemed exactly the right thing to do. Since nearly the hour afterward, she had been assailed by doubts. She had even thought the next morning of telling Francis that she had changed her mind yet again, but since she had already informed Crispin of her intent and asked him to send the notice ending their betrothal to the papers and had told her startled family of the change, it had seemed unbearably humiliating to admit that she was a complete fool who never knew her mind. Even she could scarce believe that she had entered into yet another pledge to marry one man when she was in love with another.

But the principal reason that she had stayed her tongue was that she did not want Crispin to know that she had only accepted Francis because she had been so upset with him. As it was, he would likely think that she simply had never stopped loving Francis and that the end of their betrothal had freed her to be with him. She could not bear having Crispin think her a fool for his sake.

Lady Carnavon had been surprised by Philippa's decision, but did not try to dissuade her from it. It would cause talk, of course, but not scandal, and she paid Philippa the undeserved compliment of assuming she knew her own mind. Aubery had shaken his head and said that he found the machinations of women beyond his comprehension. He added that it was enough to turn a fellow into a monk, but neither had he counseled her against marrying Francis. It was only Lianna who had seemed genuinely concerned with Philippa's decision. She, too, had listened in silence, her lovely green eyes growing wider at each sentence. "But why on earth would you wish to marry Francis?" she asked when Philippa had finished, her puzzlement obvious.

Philippa smiled a little, recalling that Lianna had never been aware of her original partiality for Francis. "He says that he loves me."

"But you cannot love him," Lianna said. "I watched you when you were with Cris and I was almost certain that you were falling in love with him."

"Crispin is a most attractive man," she allowed. "For a time I think I had a *tendre* for him. But even you said that you thought he would be a wretched husband, so you should be happy for me that I have found a means of ending my connection to him."

"I think that if Crispin were in love he would be quite different," Lianna said reflectively.

Philippa ignored this, saying, "I have always been very fond of Francis and I think we shall do quite well together."

Lianna was not convinced. "You are not so fickle in

your interests. I can't believe you would wish to marry Francis if you were in love with Crispin. Something must have occurred to change your mind. I wish you would tell me."

They were seated on Lianna's bed at Carnavon House on the night of the day that Lady Carnavon had discovered her necklace missing. They were both clad in thin, silk nightdresses, for the weather was unusually balmy. Philippa smiled and reached across the counterpane to take Lianna's hand. "If it is anything, it is that I have come to my senses. Just because you could not like Francis for a husband does not mean that I could not."

"I wish I had not come to you with that stupid letter and asked you to help me," the younger girl said with feeling. "For it affected me not at all but your life has been turned upside down ever since. Aubery is right," she concluded unhappily, "I do have more hair than wit."

"If Aubery said so to you, it was very unkind of him," Philippa replied. "And if you are looking again to blame yourself for my problems, you may set your mind at rest. Perhaps I shall quite like being a political wife. I have quite made up my mind to be happy in my future."

And so she did, in spite of her doubts. She could no longer, as she once had, imagine her life with Francis with excitement and anticipation, but she supposed she would find contentment enough if she were determined upon it.

It was the immediate future that Philippa found hard to look upon with equanimity. She felt very awkward about being married from Doremire Abbey, which was Crispin's home, but Francis had insisted upon it and Lady Carnavon concurred, saying that it would be the most natural thing and occasion the least talk. It was a scant two days after she had broken with Crispin that she found herself on the road to Doremire with her aunt and cousin, and at times there was for Philippa a quality of unreality about all of their plans.

Francis was remaining in town for about another sennight to take care of some pressing business and to procure the special license with which they would marry. Aubery, too, had elected to remain in town until the wedding, so it was only the women who journeyed to Shropshire. When they finally arrived at the abbey, the time seemed to drag endlessly and in the days following she had far too much leisure to pursue her unwelcome thoughts.

They had arrived on Tuesday and Francis accompanied by Aubery joined them earlier than expected on the following Saturday, which was a week precisely to the day on which the wedding was planned. Philippa's sense of unreality in the events that were going forward increased. She could scarcely believe that so much turmoil had occurred in her previously placid life and that it all spanned no more than a five-week period. It seemed to her that she had lived as many years in that short time.

Francis was flatteringly attentive and Philippa responded to him as if she were determined to be in love with him again, but if that were the case, it hadn't happened by midweek. And the truth was that Francis did not help his cause by seldom missing an opportunity to disparage his brother. It seemed to Philippa that he recalled every peccadillo that could be laid at Crispin's blame since they had been in short coats together, almost as if he were trying to convince her that she had done exactly the right thing to jilt Crispin and marry him. He spoke of the theft of the diamonds frequently and each time with more conviction of his brother's guilt. She and Lady

Carnavon had persuaded him that it was in the best interests of the entire family to keep the matter from spreading abroad, but apparently he saw no harm in discussing it with her. Philippa, who would have liked to forget that day completely, heartily wished he would not, but did not like to seem too particular by requesting him not to do so.

On the following Monday Philippa's own maid, Susan, made to comment on Lord Carnavon's disgrace, and Philippa, alarmed that some garbled version of the story might be circulating among the servants, forced the embarrassed abigail to tell her in great detail all of the gossip concerning herself and Crispin that was circulating in the servant's hall and to divulge to her its source. Philippa at first suspected that her aunt's dresser, Walker, had a loose tongue, but Susan surprised her by insisting that it was Coapy, Lord Francis' man, who had spoken of the matter.

Philippa found this particularly upsetting and her concern wss not allayed by the girl's assurance that it had been a private conversation and was not gossiped over in the servants hall, for if Coapy had told Susan, he might as easily have told others. There could be no doubt that he had had the story either from Walker or from his master, and Philippa decided that it was important that she knew which of them had been indiscreet.

The weather held fine, and since his arrival, Philippa and Francis had ridden out on the estate each morning after breakfast. Raised largely at Maverly, Philippa had been in the saddle a good part of her life, but Francis was an indifferent rider, so their rides were not the exercise that Philippa usually preferred but a leisurely diversion. This allowed much time for private conversation between them, which a scant two months ago would have delighted Philippa beyond measure. Now at times she found her intimacy with Francis a bit oppressive because she found she really had little to say to him, which scarcely boded well for the harmony of their future together. She was glad enough to have a definite subject to broach even if the topic were not an entirely pleasant one.

"I was rather disturbed last night," she said to Francis as they walked their horses beneath the cool canopy of tall trees in the home wood. "My Susan said something that made it obvious that she knew of the missing diamonds. Charlotte did not wish it made known at all and would be even more upset than I if she thought that gossip about it was circulating among the servants."

"I've always thought it pointless to try to have secrets from servants myself," Francis said with no show of concern. "There are times when I swear any man knows more about me than I know myself."

"I would appear that he knows about the diamonds, in any case. Susan told me that she had the story from him."

Francis only shrugged. "The truth will out, I suppose."

"It will if we are indiscreet," Philippa said caustically. "What particularly concerned me was that he hinted to Susan that an article belonging to Cris was found in or near the jewel case. Aunt Charlotte particularly adjured me to say nothing of any damning evidence against Cris because she did not wish it known that she suspected that he had taken the necklace."

"If Cris is found out, it is quite his own fault for being so careless."

"How can you say so?" Philippa asked, shocked by his heartless attitude toward the reputation of his brother. "If you do not care what is said of Cris for his own sake, you ought to care for the sake of your name."

"Cris has never had a care for his name. This is only the latest and worst scrape he has gotten himself into. You know as well as I that it is next to impossible to avoid some talk whenever anything untoward occurs."

"In this case, since it is only you and I and Aunt Charlotte who know about the necklace and her suspicions of Cris, it wants only our discretion to keep the matter contained," she said severely.

"Aren't your forgetting Walker?" he asked. "Wasn't she with Charlotte when she discovered the theft and the opal in the jewel case?"

Philippa could not help flinching slightly at the bald use of the word "theft." Both she and Lady Carnavon were careful to always describe the diamonds as "missing." "Yes, but Aunt Charlotte was able to keep her from seeing the opal and, in any case, surely Walker would not choose to speak to the other servants about the incident. She was responsible for the care of Charlotte's jewels and some suspicion is bound to fall upon her."

Francis shrugged again. His tone suggested that he was becoming bored by the conversation. "Perhaps she feels that the evidence is great enough against another."

"Perhaps," Philippa agreed reluctantly. "But it was not Walker who told Susan; I was your man, Coapy."

"Walker no doubt told him."

"You never mentioned the matter to your servant?" Philippa pressed.

"I may have, I can't recall," was Francis' response. "What the devil difference does it make? Everyone knew something was up the minute you broke off with

Cris and he was all but banished from his own house. The truth may be better than uneducated imaginings."

Philippa could not agree, but she saw that it was pointless to argue with Francis, whose careless attitude toward his brother's reputation she found repugnant. It was with some difficulty that she continued her ride with him in harmony and she cut it short with the excuse of promising to help her aunt in the stillroom.

Without even bothering to change out of her habit, she sought out her aunt and found her, as she had thought she would, enmeshed in housewifely concerns in the stillroom.

"I thought you were out riding with Francis," was the dowager's greeting. She sighed. "I have always particularly liked this stillroom," she said with a wave of her hand toward the shelves on which books on housewivery and cooking nestled with studied carelessness next to jars of preserved fruit and dried spices. "Puttering about in here was the one thing I should have missed when I handed over my keys to you." She clapped a hand over her mouth as if to physically stem her careless words. "Oh, dear, how insensitive I am to say such a thing to you."

"I do not regard it, Aunt," Philippa assured her, her mind concerned with other things than regret that she would never be chatelaine of Doremire Abbey. "I wish to have a word with you about something that concerns me. It would appear that the servants have gotten hold of the entire story of the missing diamonds, and though my abigail assures me that it is not generally discussed belowstairs, it is only a matter of time before it will be and from there it may well pass on to the world."

Lady Carnavon looked at her blankly. "Whatever

do you mean, my dear? If you are suggesting that Walker has been telling our business in the servants' hall, I can assure you you are mistaken. It was she who begged me to say nothing of the matter to anyone lest it reflect poorly on her character, for, you know, most people find it easiest to blame the servants when anything of value is missing."

Except in this family, Philippa thought, but she said, "I am not entirely certain of the source of the talk, but Susan not only knew that the diamonds were missing, she knew that the opal from Cris' ring had been found in an incriminating way."

The dowager looked thunderstruck. "She could not know that," Lady Carnavon insisted. "At least, not unless you have been indiscreet. *I* have told no one at all but you about the opal, Pip, upon my honor, not even Walker knows of it. Carnavon, of course, would not speak of it."

It was Philippa's turn to stare blankly. "But neither have I," she said positively. She had said nothing at all to Lianna about the theft and quite deliberately had given none of the details to Francis when she had told him of it. She bit her lip in consternation as she tried to recall if she had made some slip in conversation with either. She could not. "You must have told Francis," she said to the dowager. "He knows about the opal and I *know* I did not mention it to him."

"I have never exchanged a word with Francis about the necklace," Lady Carnavon insisted.

Philippa's brow was creased. "But he knows more than I told him about it."

The dowager put down the jelly jar she had been wrapping and looked intently at Philippa. "How could he?"

Philippa bit at her lip and her frown deepened. "The person who left the opal in the drawer would know of it," she said tentatively, watching for her aunt's reaction to these words.

"Do you mean Carnavon?" the dowager said cautiously. She willfully refused to understand the implications of Philippa's words. "He is very foolish to speak of it himself."

"You know I do not mean Cris."

Lady Carnavon's face was almost a comic study of consternation. "You think that Coapy took the necklace?" she said hopefully.

"No, I do not. Would he be speaking of the theft openly if he were the one who had taken the diamonds?"

"Who, then?" the dowager asked, but reluctantly, as if she did not really wish to hear the answer. Philippa made no reply but held her eyes in a steady gaze that she could not seem to avoid. At last Lady Carnavon sighed deeply and said, though clearly loath to do so, "You mean Francis. But why would he do such a thing? It would make little sense. He has his annuity from his mother and an allowance from the estate and never seems to live above his income."

"Gain may not have been his motive," Philippa said, her voice becoming hard. She still held her crop in one hand, and as anger began to overtake her, she swatted the table edge with enough force to make her aunt jump. "If it were only that the diamonds were gone, I might not think it of Francis, but it is clear that Cris is meant to take the full brunt of the blame. Not even for the sake of the Glennon name is he to be spared," she added fiercely.

"Then how can you think it would be Francis? He would surely not wish it to be made known for the disgrace it would bring any more than would Carnavon."

"Because Francis is envious of Cris. There are times when I think he hates him."

"My dear, do not let your thoughts run away with you," Lady Carnavon pleaded, fearful of where her niece's suspicions might lead her. "It is no more than a theory based on our own faulty memories. Perhaps I *did* mention the opal to Walker after all, or you may have inadvertently told Francis. It would be very wrong for us to jump to conclusions."

"But isn't that what we have already done?" Philippa asked, standing upright and moving about the room with quick steps, slashing her crop at passing objects to vent her rage. "We were meant to believe that Cris stole the necklace, and on the least bit of evidence he is thoroughly condemned."

"But it was the opal from his own ring that we found," the dowager said plaintively. "Why would we imagine it was someone else who had put it there? And Francis was not even there when Crispin made those remarks about the necklace and his gaming debts. He could not know that we would find that telling against his brother when we discovered the necklace missing."

"He may have known of some gaming debts that Cris had, though," Philippa persisted. "Or he may not have known at all, but thought that the evidence of the opal and the fact that Crispin had a key to the jewel case would be enough to damn him."

"How did Francis get into the jewel case?" Lady Carnavon said with triumph.

This did give Philippa pause. Some of the martial light died out of her eyes. "I don't know," she owned. "But they were his mother's jewels before they were yours and she may have given him a key at some time that we do not know about."

Lady Carnavon remained unconvinced. "It is all too

absurd. I cannot imagine Francis doing such a thing."

"But it is easy to believe that Cris would do it," Philippa said angrily.

The dowager insisted that she did not wish to believe it of either man and that it was only the evidence of her eyes and ears that had made her convict Crispin, and then she flatly refused to discuss the matter further. Try as she might, Philippa could not persuade her to confront Francis with the knowledge he should not have had and ask him how he had gained it.

Going up to her room to change, Philippa was less than happy about her aunt's refusal to see matters exactly as she did, but neither was she yet ready to stand up to Francis herself with her suspicions. In her first heat she wished to do just that, but her common sense warned her that it would be wiser to say nothing until she was moved less by outrage and more by calm self-command.

The evidence against Francis might be far more circumstantial than it was against Crispin, but Philippa was completely sure that she was right. It was certainly sufficiently to convince her that she could never marry Francis, whatever scandal this might engender. She had said this to her aunt, who had responded with horror. A second jilting in less than a fortnight was not to be thought of! This, coupled with her earlier peccadillo and short-lived betrothal to Crispin, would leave her reputation in irreparable tatters. Philippa understood this but still did not care. She felt that most of her problems in the past month had been made only worse by concerning herself with what the world would say, and as far as she was concerned, at this point, the world could go hang. She knew she would rather be married to the chimney sweep than to the man who had so short a time ago been her first and only love.

Once the tiny buttons at the back of her habit had been unfastened and the heavy amber cloth removed from her slender frame, Susan was dismissed with a reminder not to gossip so that Philippa could be alone to think what she should do to exonerate Crispin and prove to her aunt that Francis was the culprit. She was now deeply ashamed that the love she had professed to feel for Crispin had not been strong enough to make her believe in him despite the evidence. She felt that it was quite unforgiveable and that the very least she could do for Crispin was to exculpate him for all blame in the theft of the diamonds. How she felt concerning his knowledge before her of her inheritance, she was not as certain.

Philippa sat down before her dressing table and began to brush out her hair, but she scarcely saw the reflection that faced her. Instead, she saw the drawn features of Crispin as he had been in the garden when he realized that she could not believe him. It was with a sort of self-torture that she remembered the tantalizing way he could look down at her with half-closed eyes, his smile lazy . . . The image nearly made her heart fail within her.

Her eyes stung with unshed tears and the picture of Crispin faded to be replaced by her own features, her unhappiness clearly etched on them. She dropped her brush and buried her face in her hands, sobbing as wretchedly as she had on the day when she had given Crispin back his betrothal ring. "You are becoming a wretched watering pot, my girl," she said aloud sternly, but it had no effect at all on allaying her wretchedness.

This was how she was found several minutes later by

Lianna, who had been about to knock on her door, but who had simply come into the room uninvited when she heard the weeping from within.

"Pip? What is it?" Lianna sat on the edge of the broad stool and put her arms around her cousin. "Is it Francis? Have you had an argument?"

Philippa made a valiant attempt to smile and brush her unhappiness off. "It is nothing, just a bout of the megrims," she said, but her swollen features gave her the lie and it took very little prompting by Lianna to finally persuade Philippa to unburden herself. She told Lianna not only her suspicions that it was Francis who had stolen the necklace but finally the whole truth of how she had first loved Francis, had agreed to become betrothed to Crispin only to awaken Francis' jealousy, and how she had come to realize that it was Crispin she loved after all.

Lianna was silent for some time after Philippa had finished speaking, and to broach the awkwardness that sometimes follows the sharing of intimacies, Philippa began to speak briskly of her intention of making the best of her situation. Lianna appeared to listen while Philippa spoke of purchasing a cottage in some remote corner of the realm and devoting herself to good books, gardening, and charitable works, but Lianna heard little of this, quite lost in her own thoughts.

"You cannot marry Francis," she said suddenly, interrupting Philippa in the middle of a sentence. "He is a perfect worm of a man and I cannot think how we have all been so deceived in him for so long. At least, I think I must have known he could not be trusted, or why didn't I fall in love with him when he wished me to do so? He is quite handsome and charming when he wishes to be, so why should I not?"

"Why not indeed?" Philippa agreed quietly. "But

you needn't fear, I shan't marry him, or anyone, I expect. Even jilts with eighty thousand pounds are not much in demand."

"It is not fair that you should be called a jilt or made to suffer for this in any way. It is monstrously unfair. You did not wish to be betrothed to Crispin in the first place, and if Francis had not persuaded you into it when you were quite vulnerable, you would never have agreed to marry him. Directly or indirectly, it is the wickedness of Francis that has made you an object of talk for common people, and it is not you who should suffer for it."

Philippa's smile was mildly sardonic. "The world will neither know the truth nor care for it. But I am not blameless, am I? I agreed to both betrothals to suit my own needs of the moment. And to think I have always prided myself on my good sense," she added bitterly.

Lianna stood obviously agitated by this. "You must not say so. You are a victim, nothing more."

Philippa laughed uncertainly. "I am not sure I care more for that than for being a fool."

"If there must be blame, then it should be laid at my door," Lianna insisted, which caused Philippa to roll her eyes heavenward.

"My dear Lia, next you shall be saying that you are the cause of Napoleon trying to overrun the world," Philippa said with a touch of exasperation.

"It is not kind in you to laugh at me, Pip," Lianna said, a faint quiver to her upper lip. "It is only that I love you and would not have you unhappy for the world."

Phililppa begged her pardon at once. "But it is nonsense, you know," she said. "If anything, you did me quite a favor by affording me my first glimpse of Francis' true character. If I was foolish enough to tumble out of love with one unsuitable man and into love with another, that can be the fault of no one but me."

But Lianna could not be made to agree and Philippa was sorry that she had confided in her, especially as she had known this might be the result. In her present state, Philippa was not up to being a comforter herself, so she suggested as gently as she could that she wished for some time alone to rest and compose herself before dinner.

"If Crispin didn't steal the diamonds, would you wish to marry him after all?"

Tears threatened to break out again, but Philippa swallowed hard and pushed them firmly away. "I don't know. We said some dreadful things to each other before he left Carnavon House. I'm not even sure I wish it even if he is innocent."

"But you cannot throw yourself away on some stupid garden or be blamed for jilting Francis," Lianna said indignantly. "He will probably tell everyone that it was all your fault just to save his own wretched face."

Philippa sighed more with resignation than with defeat. "I cannot help what Francis will say, nor, at this moment, at least, do I care."

Lianna left her cousin to her rest, but when Aubery found Lianna a full hour later curled in a chair in the library, an unopened book resting in her lap, she was still deep in thought about Philippa's dilemma. "If you cared about someone and felt it was quite your fault that they were unhappy, wouldn't you try to do all you could to make them come about right again?" she asked him as soon as he came into the room.

Aubery, who to combat his boredom at being away from town during the height of the Season was even willing to find an improving book to while away the long hours, answered her that he supposed he would, but in an offhand way, his principal concern being for the shelf of books whose titles he was perusing.

"You would not flinch from what you perceived to be your duty in the matter, however difficult or extreme it might seem?" Lianna continued, seeking courage in his support.

"Of course not," he replied, and pulled out a book on ancient cultures that looked to have a number of interesting plates, if nothing else.

"And if there were some risk involved, it could only be considered an insignificant price to pay for putting things to right." Her questions were becoming firmer and more like statements.

Aubery was flipping through the pages of the book, pausing to read a passage here and there, but he was becoming aware that something more than half an ear was required of him. He slid the book back into place and turned to Lianna, his brow knit. "What needs putting to right?"

"Everything that is wrong," Lianna replied evasively. She got up and handed him the novel that she had had in her lap. "I shouldn't think you'd like this," she said in a cryptic way, and because it was not at all out of character for his cousin to be vague, Aubery simply took the book from her and replaced it on a nearby shelf, never giving their conversation another thought.

When Philippa gained control over her agitated emotions, she knew she behaved with wisdom by not acting as precipitously with Francis as she had with Crispin. She had been reasonably sure of Crispin's guilt and was only too aware that she had managed to convince herself with equal surety of Francis' culpability with no more than her own suspicions to condemn him. It was impossible not to recall her consistently erroneous judgments of both Francis and Crispin, and this sapped her confidence in her discernment. One of the Glennon brothers was a liar, a cheat, and a thief, and this time she knew she had to be certain which it was.

The only thing of which she was absolutely certain was that she could not marry Francis should he prove as innocent and unsullied as first snow. Yet for the moment she held her peace. They were not to be wed until Saturday, and knowing that Francis' principal motive in wishing to marry her was self-interest, she had no compunction about crying off at the last possible minute. It was not only that she wished the time to sort out her thoughts, if there was the least chance that she could prove to herself more concretely that Francis was the culprit who had taken the necklace, she needed the time to discover it, preferably without arousing his suspicion.

Throughout the next two days, she frequently returned to the subject of the missing diamonds whenever she and Francis were in conversation, but he never gave himself away any further and the only suspicious thing she could note was that he always turned the subject as quickly as he could to safer ground.

On one occasion, when he was gone into the village, Philippa, with the help of Susan, who kept Coapy occupied in light flirtation belowstairs, went the length of searching his bedchamber and sitting room to see if he had stashed away the jewels there. She had all but convinced herself that this was the reason that he had so insisted that they be married from Doremire, so that he would have a place to rid himself of the necklace. She knew the diamonds were far too well known for him to have safely sold them, and she would never believe that Francis would have the self-possession to cast such a valuable piece into the Thames. Neither did she believe that he would have left the diamonds behind in London, where some zealous housemaid could accidentally unearth them.

But her search proved quite fruitless and she found it extremely distasteful. Going through the private belongings of someone without his permission was unpalatable to her, and if she was disappointed that she had not discovered the necklace, she was relieved when the search was done.

Her failure did not convince her of Francis' innocence, but only made her suppose that he was either more clever or more venal than she had suspected. Either he had salted away the diamonds in an unimpeachable hiding place within the house, or he had found a means of disposing of them on the market without risk to himself. She began to fear the latter might well be true, for it would not only rid him of the incriminating presence of the necklace, but also gain him a few thousand pounds as well.

But thoughts such as these were best not fostered, for they set Philippa's blood to boil and made her fingers itch to box Francis' ears whenever she beheld him. Yet while any doubt or possibility of resolving it with certainty remained, she knew she would be wisest to say nothing, swallowing all ire and confiding none of her intentions. If nothing else, Doremire Abbey was a large house and there were still many places she could search for the diamonds whenever she could manage to be unobserved.

Lady Carnavon went on as if she and Philippa had never had that conversation in the stillroom, and when she observed her niece conducting herself in a similar manner, she supposed that Philippa had rethought her suspicions and was glad of this. For though she did not like to think so basely of Crispin, it was easier to do so than to believe that his brother was of even more reprehensible character.

Lianna once or twice tried to steer conversation with Philippa to her suspicions and what she meant to do with them, but Philippa was consistently evasive, and after a while Lianna did not press her, contenting herself with watching her cousin with pensive eyes, which was wont to make Philippa feel torn between amusement and annoyance.

But her cousin's pensiveness made Philippa fear that Lianna meant to see what information she herself could get from Francis. She feared this might arouse his suspicions, so whenever she could manage it, she maneuvered Aubery into taking Lianna on rides about the park, driving her into Doremire to match ribbons and other such diversions to keep the young girl occupied. Her aunt, observing this, accused her of matchmaking, but Philippa only laughed and said that while they continued to squabble like children, she had no fear of Lianna and Aubery falling in love.

If Francis supposed that Philippa had any suspicions, he did not show that he thought so. He was in all things considerable and attentive, exactly as Philippa, only a short time before, had always dreamed he would be when at last they could declare their love openly. It continually astonished her that her dreams could have changed so much, but she had no regrets for this. She even thought, quite cynically, that the principal reason for Francis' excellent demeanor was that all events were falling out exactly as he intended them, and had nothing at all to do with his feelings for her. A residue of bitterness for the heart Francis had betrayed made her not at all sorry to think what his reaction would be when she at last told him that she did not mean to marry him.

They kept early hours at Doremíre Abbey. This was
not a lively house party with numerous daytime
activities and gay evening entertainments to while
away the hours. For a visit that was scheduled to end
with a wedding the atmosphere was positively dour.
Most nights the entire household was abed well before
midnight, with the arrival of the tea tray in the with-
drawing room after dinner signaling Francis' and
Aubery's departure for a final bit of brandy before
retiring. It was seldom long after this that the ladies
retired to their bedchambers as well.

Though Philippa might spend much of her time
during the day pondering her unresolved feelings for
Crispin and the truth of the missing diamonds, she was
blessed with the gift of being able to empty her mind
of all troubles when she needed rest. Despite any
daytime turmoil, her sleep was untroubled. Her bedchamber was in the family wing across from Lianna's
and the first after the stairs on the same side of the hall
as Francis' rooms.

Francis might be given to philandering, but
Philippa would not have described him as a man of
strong passions, and thus, though her bedchamber
shared a connecting door with his sitting room, she
had never felt any need to formally ascertain that that
door was firmly bolted. Yet, when she was awakened
near midnight by some indefinable sound, her first
thought was that Francis had stayed up too late with
the brandy bottle and was seeking to cement his
position with her by seduction or worse.

She sat up in bed, her heart pounding, her eyes fixed
wide in the direction of the door, but the door did not
open and the sound, whatever it may have been, was
not repeated. After a few minutes, she felt rather
foolish, but she could not quite tell herself that it had
only been part of a dream. Some instinct told her that

something was amiss even if her waking conjecture had been false.

Casting the sheets aside, Philippa slid out of bed and tiptoed across the room in her bare feet to put her ear against the connection door. The silence was absolute, but she was not satisfied. She next went to her window, which overlooked a portion of the drive that led to the stables, but saw not so much as a wavering shadow. It was the oddest thing, but she could not quite shake a slight feeling of disappointment. She had not the slightest wish for Francis' attentions and certainly would have been in a quake if she believed that burglars were in the house, but when she had awakened, every fiber of her being had come alive to the notion that "something" was about to happen and now she had an irrational sense of being let down.

Philippa walked back to her bed but she did not crawl back between the sheets. She found her slippers and donned these and her dressing gown and then went out into the dark hall. Not the tiniest glimmer of light shone from under any of the doors. But, in spite of her expectations, she was nearly startled into a gasp when the door nearest to hers, the one leading into Francis' sitting room, suddenly swung inward and a man stepped into the hall only a few feet away from her. It was a moonless night and the hall boasted only one window at its far end, so the darkness was nearly complete; yet, even so, she knew the man was no servant and assumed it was Francis, bent on some dark purpose, she was certain. He saw her at once and caught his breath. As well he might, Philippa thought grimly, her mind working rapidly how she might use this to her advantage to gain knowledge of the necklace or to end her connection with him.

But he moved swiftly, taking her by the arm in a manner that was not very gentle and drawing her back into her room quickly, silently closing the door behind them. She pulled herself away from his grasp. "I suppose you are meeting some serving girl," she said cuttingly, not bothering to lower her voice. "Clandestine romance seems to be your forte."

"I've had my moments," he admitted, and Philippa knew at once by his voice that once again in the dark, she had mistaken one Glennon brother for the other.

"Cris!" A variety of emotions seemed to flow through her simultaneously; the safest to focus on was her astonishment. Whatever his feelings in the matter, she had never supposed that he would come to Doremire to see her wed to his brother.

He put two fingers to her lips and, taking her arm again, led her over to the bed. She sat down on the side of it without thinking, but when he joined her, she felt the impropriety, or more accurately, the danger, of the situation and stood again, but he pulled her down and advised her in a matter-of-fact way not to be missish. "Although your gown awakens my lasciviousness, I have certainly not ridden half the night in the pitch black just to ravish you, my love," he said in his dry way. "Later, perhaps, when this coil is unraveled. Or did you think I was Francis come to do it?" he said with perception. "I know you hate me now, Pip, but please, don't let it be enough to marry Francis to spite me. He isn't for you, my dear, whatever you may have convinced yourself of."

"My decision to marry Francis had nothing to do with you," she said pointedly. "It is only your vanity that would have it so."

"Beautiful liar," he said softly, touching her cheek with the back of one finger. "You aren't in love with Francis."

She stood abruptly and said with more heat than she intended, "Nor with you!"

"Ah, but you are no longer going to marry me."

Philippa knew this all too well; her heart was heavy with it. She would not marry Crispin, could not marry Francis; she wished with all her heart that she had never known either man. "No. I am certainly not going to marry *you*," she said, raising her chin. She would not wear her heart on her sleeve. Even if Crispin had not stolen the diamonds, she still was unconvinced that he, too, had not made love to her to his purpose. It would take more than a few soft words or enticing caresses to rebuild her trust in him.

"I know you can't believe in me, Pip," he said. "Why should you, when all who know me best warn you against me and ever Charlotte, who has always liked me better than most, turns against me? As soon as I recovered my temper, I realized it wasn't fair to expect it of you. Then I knew the only thing for me to do was to prove to you on at least one head that I was not a liar and worse. I can prove that I didn't take that damned necklace."

Philippa looked down at him and was very glad of the cover of darkness, for she was sure that the sudden surge of hope that she felt must have shown in her eyes. She mattered enough to him that he would ride *ventre à terre* to prove himself in her eyes. But the hope was yet tempered by the fear that it was only words to persuade her again to him. "What is it?" she asked cautiously.

"Not what, but who. And I do not intend to tell you. My proof will be here tomorrow, by late morning I am hoping, if the London mail is not late."

"Someone is arriving on the mail?"

"I've told you too much already," he said, dropping his voice to a stagy whisper. "It is not that I don't trust you, beauty, but I have always found that my schemes profit most when I keep my counsel. We shall have a splendid little scene—in the library, I think, leather and velvet will heighten the sense of drama."

"Why are you here now, then?" she asked baldly. "Unless you can speak at once, you will make it very awkward for everyone."

"I certainly intend to make it awkward for someone," he said with a short laugh, and then added suddenly, "When are you to marry Francis?"

With a start, Philippa realized that it was already the eve of her wedding. "Tomorrow. Saturday, that is," she replied.

"I didn't think you would be wed before the end of the week, but I wanted to be here in case," he said. "I have every belief that tomorrow will prove my innocence, but I want you to promise me that if it is delayed for any reason, you will not marry Francis until you have seen my proof."

"Even if it proved indefinite in arriving?" she said with a small sneer.

"It won't," he said shortly. "I could not convince my 'proof' to journey with me tonight. Actually," he admitted, "I did not intend to arrive until tomorrow, either. I thought to put up for the night at the Boar's Head in Doremire, but my blasted horse cast a shoe just out of Knoxbury and by the time I had it seen to, the Boar's Head was dark and quiet, and rather than make a fuss that might set tongues wagging, I thought it best just to come here. I have no intention of bounding into the breakfast room tomorrow to the astonishment of all. I shall slip out of the house again without being seeen."

"What were you doing in Francis' sitting room?" she asked, and knew that he was not pleased by the question.

"Are you disappointed, my dear?" he said, and even in the dark she could tell that he was smiling at her in his lazy, tantalizing way. "Were you hoping it was Francis come to ravish you?"

It proved an effective means of deflecting her, if that was his intention. "I think you had better leave," she said frigidly. She stood and waited for him to follow suit.

He did, but he simultaneously leaned forward and kissed her lightly before she could resist. "I'll see Francis in hell before I'll let him have you," he said, entirely without menace, but with an intensity that both chilled and excited her. Then he left her in this state, melting into the shadows of the hall again, and was gone before she could admit even to herself that with all her heart she wished he had stayed.

10

Philippa did not know what to expect when she went down for breakfast the next morning. She had been up and dressed even before her usual early hour and she knew it was in anticipation of what this day would bring. She was the first to enter the breakfast room, surprising the servants who were still setting out the first dishes on the sideboard. She was soon followed by her brother and Lianna, both early risers themselves; her aunt, who only slept late when keeping odd hours in town; and finally Francis, up much before his usual time from having retired early out of sheer boredom.

Philippa kept glancing at the doorway from time to time half-expecting Crispin to bound into the room as he had suggested. What dramatics the day promised would obviously be put off until after the arrival of the mail at Doremire, and she would just have to contain her impatience until then as best she could.

Philippa risked a few discreet questions to Francis, who might possibly have heard Crispin in his sitting room, as she had, but Francis seemed curiously distracted this morning and was even a little brusque when replying to her so that Philippa wondered if even in spite of the prize of her inheritance, her erstwhile "lover" was not coming down with a case of cold feet. A man so versed at ingratiating himself with her sex while avoiding all commitment must have some pause at the thought of being bound at last even with eighty thousand pounds to soften the bounds. She wished she might assure Francis at once that he had no cause for concern.

After breakfast Philippa declined an offer from her brother to take her for a drive into the village, instead again suggesting Lianna as a substitute. Philippa herself offered to help her aunt, who was embroidering altar cloths for the chapel so that she would be sure to be close at hand when Crispin returned. The minutes registered like hours to Philippa and she proved glad of the occupation. Every time she heard the least sound from outside the house, she thought it Crispin, arrived at last with his proof. When she was not starting at noises or glancing at the door, she was keeping a surreptitious eye on the mantel clock, which told her the morning was all but gone. Her hope began to fade a bit and she began to wonder if he had really meant what he had said the night before. Any of it.

Lady Carnavon, aware of her restlessness, asked her more than once if there were anything the matter, but Philippa replied negatively and she eventually put it down to prenuptial jitters, hardly surprising in the circumstances.

She bore patiently Philippa's obvious impatience until a footman entered their parlor where they sat with their needlework and announced that luncheon was awaiting their pleasure.

"I hope you are not still thinking of that absurd conversation we had the other day about Francis," she said bracingly. "I am persuaded you do not really think he could be so wicked. If it is giving you doubts about the wedding, you must just put it out of your mind, for you will only make yourself wretched if you do not."

Philippa supposed that unless she meant to speak at the very altar, the time had come to disabuse her aunt of the notion that the wedding between her and Francis would take place tomorrow, but she hesitated to do so until Crispin had arrived with his "proof." Only, as time passed, she had less and less faith in this and wondered if it mightn't just be best to unburden herself to her aunt at once. But she was saved having to make this decision at once by the arrival of Lianna and Aubery, who had returned from their drive for luncheon.

Francis joined them not long afterward and they enjoyed their midday meal without interruption, dramatic or otherwise. Philippa half-began to wonder if she had dreamed her meeting with Crispin the previous night and started to think up excuses to ride into Doremire to the Boar's Head herself.

She was just returning to the house from a restless stroll about the garden, careful not to stray too far from the house, when at last the first sounds of some sort of domestic uproar were heard in the halls of Doremire Abbey. She hastened her steps, angry that she should have missed what must have been a most dramatic entrance when Crispin had arrived.

But the sounds she heard as she came into the house were not quite what she had expected: a woman's voice—Lianna's, she thought—was raised in shrill, urgent accents, and two footmen and Johnson himself raced past her across the entrance hall and into the east wing, from which the cries had come.

Philippa, still expecting to find Crispin's arrival at the bottom of the turmoil, followed them, quickening her pace. Several other servants joined the parade, and following hard on their heels was Aubery. Lady

Carnavon entered the hall from the opposite direction, and she was joined by two or three housemaids. The male servants and the dowager reached the library in a dead heat. Johnson, his alarm making him quite forget his place, pushed open the ajar door and rushed into the room ahead of her ladyship. Philippa came up behind him, literally elbowing her way through the crowd that was gathered about the doorway. The bottleneck was the result of astonishment. All of the company ended their flight to stand and gape.

Crispin was nowhere to be seen, but Francis was there, his face very red and his expression hunted. Lianna looked wide-eyed and frightened and her gown was a little torn on the bodice near the sleeve. Lady Carnavon hurried into the room and went at once to her daughter's side.

As soon as her audience was assembled, Lianna rolled up her eyes and swooned gracefully into a convenient sofa. The dowager called at once for burned feathers and hartshorn. All eyes focused on Francis, who was looking about with quick, darting glances as if seeking a means of escape.

It was Aubery who finally spoke. "What the devil's going on? I'm beginning to think this whole damn family's escaped from Bedlam." He glared at Francis in a stony, belligerent way.

"It—it's nothing," Francis said quickly in a far-from-steady voice. "A misunderstanding."

"Nothing?" Lianna said scathingly, recovering timely from her swoon. She turned flashing eyes and heaving bosom toward Lord Francis Glennon. "*I* do not call rape nothing."

There was a collective gasp and Aubery's hand balled into fists. His sister laid a restraining hand on his arm, but he shrugged it off. He took a menacing step toward Francis, who backed off in equal measure.

"It was no such thing, I assure you," he said, his voice rising to an unpleasantly high pitch. "Damn it Lia, you know it was no such thing."

"I was foolish enough to believe you when you said you wished for a private word with me on a family matter," the young girl responded with bitter self-recrimination. "It is obvious that we have all of us been deceived in you, especially my poor Philippa," she added, dabbing at her eyes with a small square of lace conveniently at hand. "But now she may see for herself what you are and be free of you at last. There is no one in the world who would condemn her giving you your congé now."

This was said with a significant glance cast at Philippa, who realized at last that these histrionics were for her benefit. She thought it would be a shame to put the opportunity to waste. "I fear Lia is right," she said dolefully, even going the length of placing a hand on her brow in mock sorrow. "It would be a very grave mistake for me to marry a man who had an attraction for another."

She had scarcely finished speaking when Aubery said hotly, "Damn your eyes, Glennon. You'll pay for this." And before anyone could stop him—assuming that anyone wished to do so—he crossed the small space that separated him from Francis and planted him a facer that left the latter prone on the floor tasting the dust in the carpet. Another gasp went about the room at this, but there was this time an element of approval in the sound. The Deceiver of Women Getting His Just Deserts is always a crowd-pleaser.

It might have been supposed that at this point the denouement had been reached and the drama played out, but to the avid interest of the assembled household yet another element of the drama appeared, this in the person of the lord and master of Doremire Abbey. Crispin entered the room in the most casual way, as if he were only returning from a ride, but his entrance was none the less dramatic for all that. The company parted for him as if doing so were a stage direction, and he strolled over to where his brother was struggling to regain his feet and his composure. "I find kicking a man when he is down deplorably bad form, Francis," he said amiably, "but all your markers are called in today, I am afraid."

Francis managed a sitting position and looked up at his brother, who immediately stood aside to reveal a smallish, sandy-haired man who had entered the room in his lordship's wake quite unnoticed. Crispin looked questioningly at the man, who in his turn was staring hard at Francis. The man looked up to Crispin and nodded briskly. Crispin's response was to smile slowly and with satisfaction.

But if the majority of the audience assumed that they were to be privy to the last act of the play and all of the Glennon family's dirty linen, they quickly learned their mistake. Taking charge of the situation, Crispin fired a few quick commands at his majordomo, who straightened his posture as he recalled his exalted position in the household. Johnson quickly rounded up his underlings and bustled them out of the room, though several of them glanced back, as they passed through the door, with obvious reluctance.

With the family finally alone, Crispin introduced the strange man as Mr. Biggens to the others in a way as casual as if he were bringing the man to tea instead of into the midst of a family imbroglio. The amenities seen to, Crispin at last condescended to explain himself. "Mr. Biggens is a moneylender who occasionally purchases items of rare value for the right price. His principal reputation lies in his extreme care for discretion, and his office is frequented by people of the highest *ton* who do not wish to publicize a temporary financial difficulty. Is that not so, Mr. Biggens?"

Mr. Biggens nodded again. He was watching Francis, who had gotten to his feet and was brushing himself off and not regarding either his brother or Mr. Biggens. "That is so," the man said with yet another nod. "Biggens prides himself on knowing how to be closemouthed. But this matter was most irregular. Felt it was my clear duty to speak plainly to his lordship when he inquired about his property."

Crispin held a velvet drawstring bag in his hand, and while Mr. Biggens spoke, he opened it and allowed the contents to cascade into his hand. Before the amazed eyes of all, the Carnavon diamonds appeared.

The others were watching Crispin and Mr. Biggens; only Philippa thought to look at Francis during all of this, and at the sight of the diamonds he blanched visibly.

"If you hope to get on in your chosen career, my dear brother," Crispin advised in his silky voice, "you are going to have to learn to cover your tracks a bit better. The art of manipulating events to your will is quite subtle. In your place, I would have consigned the value of the stones to the devil and made certain that they could never be found again or traced to me." He held up the necklace in front of Francis, who looked at it as if it were a serpent coiled to strike.

"I don't know what the devil you're talking about," Francis said with what was obvious to everyone was bluster.

"Ho," said Aubery with relish. "So that's your

game. Philanderer, rapist, and thief as well. We're probably lucky you haven't slit our throats in the night."

"Don't be absurd, Aubery," his aunt advised him. "I think both Crispin and Francis have some explaining to do and we shall go on far more comfortably if we abandon this silly posture of melodrama." She very deliberately sat herself on the sofa next to Lianna, who had quite forgotten her vapors as soon as Crispin had arrived. After a reluctant pause—melodrama has its attractions—the others followed her lead, placing themselves on the sofas and chairs that formed a conversational grouping in the room. Without seeming to do so deliberately, everyone avoided the chair nearest to Francis, as if they had already passed judgment on him and determined him a pariah.

Mr. Biggens sat on the edge of a straight-backed chair, looking supremely uncomfortable, and Crispin alone remained standing. "I shall do the credit, dear boy," he said, addressing Francis, "of assuming that manipulation *was* your principal motive for taking the necklace. You took the money Mr. Biggens gave to you for the diamonds, but what mattered to you was that I be blamed for the theft and that Philippa lose what little trust in me she still possessed."

Francis, cast dreadfully off balance by Lianna's histronics, Aubery's physical assault, and his brother's accusations, found his mental capacities taxed to the limit. His normally nimble mind failed him and explanations eluded him, for he scarcely knew which charge to answer first. He fell back on a lame attempt to cast the blame elsewhere. "It won't work, Cris. Everyone knows you took the necklace yourself. Trying to blame me won't wash; my credit will stand against yours at any time."

Crispin looked around the room from one attentive

face to the other in a very deliberate way. "Will it, I wonder? Yet—correct me if I err—your credit did not appear to be in very good order even before I arrived."

"He tried to ravish me," Lianna said at this cue, the suggestion of a sob returning to her voice.

"Damn it! It was no such thing, and you know it," Francis cried, goaded. "*You* lured me in here. You wanted me to think . . ." He broke off as he saw the look of disgust pass on his stepmother's face. "That is," he hastily amended, "I thought you wished for my . . ." His explanations only placed him in a worse light, and having the sense to realize this, he abandoned the attempt. "What is the point? You have already judged me, haven't you?" he said, addressing no one in particular. "I suppose it is his doing," he added, pointing an accusatory finger at his brother. "*He* has always been a philanderer and a liar with scant care for his own honor or that of the family. Is it such a step that he should steal an entailed necklace to pay off his debts so that he can trick a gullible heiress into believing his lies? How the devil can you believe him, a damned libertine, over me?"

Crispin seemed not the least put out by the viciousness of his brother's attack. He even smiled. "Vilification of my character won't whitewash yours, dear brother," he said easily. He turned to Mr. Biggens, who seemed a little startled to be addressed again. "Who brought you the diamonds for sale, Mr. Biggens?"

The man cleared his throat and began to speak in a tone that suggested a recital of a story he had told before. "A fortnight or so ago a gentleman most well spoken and well dressed came to me presenting himself as his lordship—that is, the Marquess of Carnavon— saying that he'd fallen on a bit of bad luck at play. He said he was due to leg-shackle himself to a chary heiress and needed a bit of the ready as quick as may be so she wouldn't get the wind up over his debts."

He paused, shifting a bit in his chair as he warmed to his story. "It's my business to know all the best pieces belonging to all the first families, and I knew the Carnavon diamonds as soon as I set my eyes on them. I did some business with his late lordship— that is, his present lordship's father—and this fellow certainly had the look of him. But his old lordship once brought his boy with him, a score of years ago. A viscount the lad was called then, so I knew it was the eldest, and he had blond curls and blue eyes as pretty as any girl could hope for. I remember thinking such pretty looks were quite wasted on a boy, so the memory of it stuck." He emphasized this by tapping a forefinger against his temple.

He paused again, eyeing his rapt audience with satisfaction. There was Crispin before them, his curls as golden as ever they had been and his eyes a clear azure as they gazed serenely upon the company. "Well, this fellow calling himself Lord Carnavon was light-haired and his eyes were blue after a fashion, but it wasn't the same, if you take me. Still, people change, and it was a good many years since I'd set my peepers on him, so I didn't think of it overmuch. Then this fellow," he continued, nodding toward Crispin, "says *he's* the Marquess of Carnavon and I took one look and never had a doubt of it. He tells me his story, and when he's done, I think to myself, Biggens, discretion is your bread and butter, but what you've got here is an ugly bit of business. So I goes to my safe where I keep a few of the special things and I gives him the necklace. I never have the famous pieces cut up straightaway, whatever the instructions. More than one client has come back within the month desperate with the hope that their property can still be repurchased."

"And *re*purchased they have been," Crispin said, tossing the diamonds in a careless way to his brother.

The look that a startled Francis cast his brother and Mr. Biggens was quite venomous, in Philippa's opinion, but it was obvious he was not yet ready to own up to his crime. "You can't believe this nonsense," he said, addressing Philippa. "You know what Carnavon's like. He probably paid this cit to concoct this story so he could exonerate himself."

Mr. Biggens sat up very straight. "That he did not do," he said stiffly. "Not everyone cares for the sort of dealing I do, but at least I always do it honest. You won't find no one to speak against the honesty of John Biggens, however far or high you was to look."

"I do not think it is your integrity my brother wishes to impugn, Mr. Biggens," Crispin said soothingly, "but his own, which he is desperately trying to salvage. Cut line, Fran," he advised his brother. "Look at the faces about you and tell me if you see anyone ready to leap to your defense."

Francis did just as he was advised. His stepmother looked angry and disappointed, Lianna contemptuous. There were obvious thunderclouds in Aubery's expression and Philippa regarded him with a coldness that made it obvious he could not count on her support either. "It had to be you that took the necklace; the opal from the ring you always wore was found in the case the diamonds were kept in."

"The ring that I had missed for a day or two and assumed mislaid," Crispin said. "I suppose you prized out the stone. It was cleverly done of you. No one would have believed that the ring could come off without my noticing, but it is easy enough to lose a stone."

"How did you know that the opal was found in the jewel case, Francis?" Philippa asked, surprising

Crispin, for he had expected no ally in her. "That detail was kept even from Walker, who was present when my aunt discovered her loss."

After the briefest hesitation Francis said, "You told me."

"I did not."

"Then it was Charlotte," he replied in a dismissive way.

"I am quite certain that I never mentioned it to you, Francis," Lady Carnavon said, unwilling to be his champion to the extent that she would lie for him. "I told no one at all of the opal except for Philippa, who was with me shortly after I found it, and Crispin himself."

"Well, one of you certainly told me; you've just forgotten," he said angrily. "What difference does it make who told me? It has nothing to do with the fact that the opal was found in the jewel case and that it belonged to Crispin, not me."

"It might if you put it there," Philippa said quietly.

Francis cast the diamonds onto the nearest table and stood abruptly. "If I put it there! Damn it, it was his ring," he said, almost shouting. "It's all damned lies. I won't be held accountable for what he's done." The expressions on the faces surrounding him were now identical: stony disbelief and accusation. Francis pointed again to his brother. "He's the liar and the cheat. You *can't* believe him over me." But it was obvious that the others could and did, and when only silence greeted his outburst, he sank back into his chair, staring sullenly at the Turkey carpet.

The silence grew and became uncomfortable. It was obvious that Francis was not going to break down and admit his guilt, and it was equally obvious that no one believed his denials. His own slip in admitting a knowledge he should not have possessed, coupled with the testimony of the disinterested Mr. Biggens, made the case against him much stronger than it had been against Crispin—too strong for lies to carry the day.

The uncomfortable aura increased and finally Philippa stood and faced Francis. "I must add to your burden, I fear. In the circumstance, you must see that I could never marry you. All that has happened today has made it certain, but I had already decided against it in any case. It was a mistake to accept your offer and I realized it almost at once." Francis started to speak but she spoke over him, saying, "Please do not add to the difficulty of this by trying to persuade me against it. I don't believe you care for me any more than I do for you. I don't believe you care overmuch for anyone but yourself. You see the world through no eyes but your own." She turned and left the room with quiet dignity, keeping her head up but deliberately not looking toward Crispin.

When she was gone, it was Lady Carnavon who was next to stand and speak. "Francis, it grieves me very much to say this, but I must admit that I, too, have been mistaken in your character. You were occasionally a selfish young man, but I never thought this of you. This is not my house, so I don't have the authority to order you out of it, but if Carnavon chooses to allow you to stay, I shall be left with no choice but to retire at once to the dower house." She picked up her necklace from the table where Francis had cast it, and gathered her skirts about her. "Lia, I shall need you to help me to write the notes putting off our neighbors for the wedding breakfast tomorrow."

Lianna was a little reluctant to leave, for she feared that the final scene had yet to play out, but she obediently followed her mother, only pausing to cast a triumphant, pitying glance at Francis as she passed him. When the door closed behind the ladies, Crispin ran for a servant, who arrived with such alacrity it was obvious that he had been lurking in the hall.

Crispin instructed the man to have a carriage readied to convey Mr. Biggens back to the Boar's Head. When the footman left, he held out his hand to Mr. Biggens, thanking him for his assistance.

Francis broke into this. "You won't get away with your lies," he said threateningly to the moneylender. "I'll see you ruined for this day's work, I promise you."

The little man sniffed. "I don't fear the likes of you. I have friends among the quality that wouldn't have *you* at their dinner tables. You and I both know it was you that came to my office on Bank Street with that necklace and that you told me you was Lord Carnavon. I got my reputation to think of, and false dealing is not what I hold with. I made it my business to find out a bit about Lord Francis Glennon, and I know you got ambitions. You make trouble for me and you'll find Biggens has the connections to give as good as he gets." With this he nodded at Aubery, shook hands in a brisk way with Crispin and left with the footman, who opportunely reentered the room at that moment to announce the arrival of the carriage.

"He's right, you know," Crispin said to his brother. "I don't want this mess published abroad, but you should want it even less, Fran. You have an allowance that is respectable and an annuity that should keep you in reasonable comfort, if not in style. And who knows, you may do better for yourself; the world is full of gullible heiresses.

"I quite agree with Charlotte that you should leave here as soon as possible," he added, "and I am afraid that you will not find yourself welcome at the London house either. There shall doubtless be some talk when it becomes obvious to the world that we are estranged, but we have never been close, so I think we may contrive to keep speculation at a minimum."

"I'll pay you out for this," Francis said in a voice that now sounded more petulant than menacing.

"You behold me atremble," Crispin replied mockingly. "You are not a fool, Francis. I think you'll realize who would be hurt the most if you make any difficulty in this matter."

Knowing he was beaten but incapable of admitting it, Francis glared impotently at his brother for a moment and then got up and slammed himself out of the room with considerable force.

Aubery had sat in a chair a little apart from the others. His principal interest in the proceedings once Crispin had arrived was that of an observer. "Bravo!" he said in a congratulatory tone. "Piqued, repiqued, and capoted. I knew he was a damned sly one when I saw the game he was playing with Pippa and Lia, but I have to admit I wouldn't have thought he'd take it to the length of stealing the Carnavon diamonds just to rout you. I wouldn't have thought he had the bottom for it. I never understood why Pip had formed such an attachment to him, but then I thought she was off her head when she wanted to marry you, too."

"She didn't precisely want to," Crispin corrected. "But neither did I . . . then."

The words he left unspoken were most eloquent. Aubery hesitated a moment before accepting a glass of madeira that Crispin had poured out for him. He raised his eyes to Crispin's. "How does Philippa feel?"

"I don't know," Crispin replied honestly, and sat down in the chair Francis had occupied. "I had begun to think that she was falling in love with me, as much as I am with her, but she has little trust in me. Given the way she was always warned against me, I cannot hold her in blame for it. My hope is not strong that she could learn to trust and love me now that she knows I am not the monster I was painted, but it is not absent."

"I think you might be optimistic. Philippa once told me that no matter how often one tumbles into love, when it is the right person, all obstacles will eventually vanish." Aubery raised his glass in salute to the older man. "May it be so for you, Cris. You don't need my consent, but you have it. I think I should like having you as my brother-in-law."

When Philippa left the library she went to her sitting room and waited. She hadn't the least doubt that Crispin would come to her, and she wished she might have the serenity to be found reading a book or plying her needle when he entered, but her agitation was too great to allow of any occupation other than pacing restlessly about the room. She still did not know what she would say to him. She could not help being excited after what he had said to her last night. He still loved her and wanted her, but did she want him? Her heart knew that she did, but her head had serious reservations. Even if he were innocent of the theft of the diamonds, there was still the matter of her inheritance and the fact that he had known of it before the night she had met him in the rose garden at Mac-Reath House. However exemplary his character, how could she be sure that her principal attraction for him was not her fortune? If it were, she had few illusions for their future. She understood perfectly that if she could not hold Crispin's heart, she would never hold his person. The wretched existence that would be her lot in that case was not to be thought of.

The light was nearly gone and her maid had already

lit a number of candles to dispel the gloom. Philippa
stood before the window looking down into the
gathering darkness, her thoughts interrupted at last by
a scratching at the door. She knew it was he; her heart
was beating very rapidly. She turned and bade him
enter.

"Do you wish to see me, Pippa?" he asked quietly as
he came into the room.

"I don't know," Philippa said with perfect honesty,
forgetting the speeches concerning her feelings and
doubts that she had concocted during her pacing.

"Do you believe the proof that I have shown you?"

"Yes. Actually, I had come to believe you innocent
before it."

He looked his surprise. "Did you? Did you believe it
before we spoke last night?"

She nodded, looking away from him. "I wasn't
certain, but I had already come to suspect Francis."

"Then it was not that you believed in me but that
you doubted him."

"No." She lifted her eyes to his for the briefest
moment before looking away again. "That is, after we
came here and I was able to think more clearly, I
found it hard to believe you would have done the thing
so stupidly."

He laughed. "If the theft had been clever, would
you have thought me guilty then?"

"If it had been managed cleverly, we should never
have suspected you in the first place," Philippa said,
looking up again and this time managing a smile.
"Francis behaved as if he wanted the theft known
outside the family. He was so obviously relishing your
ruin that I could not acquit him of disinterest."

Crispin sighed. "He can be quite Machiavellian in
his thinking. I almost think it was a pity that he was

not firstborn. In my place he would have used his position to advantage and likely would be lord chancellor now and a duke into the bargain."

"I wonder Francis did not attach himself to an heiress long before I received my legacy."

"Oh, he tried from time to time," Crispin said, "but, you see, a younger son with no more than a competence and no certain future in his chosen career has so little to bargain with. I never fancied he was particularly adept at making up to your sex. Or was he?"

Philippa shook her head. "Not as you are," she said, unable to resist a quizzing tone. "But I hardly know what he was. The image that I had of Francis was that of an ideal. The ideal of a schoolgirl. I made excuses for his every divergence from that ideal rather than abandon it. My only consolation must be that no one else realized how devious and self-seeking he could be, except perhaps you."

"I have known him the whole of his life, an advantage—or disadvantage, depending on how one views it." He smiled faintly. "But I don't believe Francis is as bad as recent events have made him seem. He *is* self-seeking, but not wicked, I think. He wanted to have his cake and eat it too, and when he saw you slipping away from him, he took what steps he had to to prevent it."

"It was my inheritance he did not wish to see slip away from him," Philippa said bitterly. "I wish that Cousin Dominic had willed his fortune to Aubery or—or the Society of Sea Gull Fanciers," she said with sudden vehemence.

"So do I," he said with equal feeling. He came up to her as if to embrace her but did not do so. He was silent until she looked up at him. "But you don't believe that, do you?"

His face was unreadable, but the expression in his eyes was intense. She wanted to pour out all the love that was in her heart to him, but she needed to believe that he wanted her only for herself. She could not do so without doubt, so she said nothing.

His expression changed and so did his voice. "Then there is little more for me to say," he said in a clipped way. "I won't embarrass us both by begging you to have me, or offend you by forcing myself on you."

"Cris," she said, some of her anguish evident. "It is not that I don't want to believe you."

"Don't bother to qualify your feelings," he said, the bitterness clear in his voice and expression. "I can't even blame you for them."

Philippa did not want to leave it at this, but tears constricted her throat and blurred her vision, and her mind seemed dense as lead. He looked down at her for a long moment as silent tears dropped from her eyes; his own hooded eyes were bright and moist. Then he left her and she did nothing to stop him.

By the following morning bucolic serenity again reigned at Doremire Abbey. Francis had left nearly with the dawn without taking leave of anyone or apprising anyone of his immediate plans. In his step-mother's opinion it was just as well. Philippa also learned from her aunt that Crispin had not been much behind him.

It was not to be supposed that Philippa did not replay the final scene between her and Crispin in her mind a thousand times. It took all her self-control, aided by the fact that she had no idea where he had gone, to keep herself from flying after him, for a sleepless, lonely night had all but convinced her that if life with Crispin would be uncertain, life without him would be insupportable.

Fortunately, much of her time, which would have been taken up in fruitless and unhappy conjecture, was occupied with undoing the preparations for the second of her weddings never to take place. Writing an extremely difficult letter to her Uncle Henry and Aunt Tess and rescinding orders to various local tradesmen kept her busy most of that day. Lady Carnavon seemed to have an endless number of domestic chores for her to accomplish on the next, while Aubery and Lianna, hoping to raise her spirits, insisted that she accompany them on a drive to visit a local ruin of some repute, and after dinner engaged her in a lively game of lottery tickets that even Lady Carnavon was not above joining. Philippa appreciated their concern and attempts to occupy her, though by Sunday morning she was glad enough of some time alone.

A very genuine headache made her cry off from attending morning services with the rest of the family, though, at least in part, her motive was a wish to avoid the curious stares of their friends who must be wondering what sort of creature became betrothed to two men who happened to be brothers and jilted both within less than a month's time. She rather wondered at the answer to this herself, unable to decide whether she was a fool, naive, or a victim of the rapacity of both men.

But in an hour's time Philippa was wishing she had braved any rude stares she might have drawn, for her thoughts inevitably turned to Crispin and the emptiness of her future without him. In the end she could not bear it and left her room for the morning room, where she went to the writing desk in the window embrasure. She ruined one page of hot-pressed foolscap after the other attempting some sort of letter to him, trying, at the least, to explain how much she wished she could believe that his love was genuine.

Philippa heard the carriage drive past beneath the windows, but merely remarked mentally that the others were returned from the service rather earlier than usual. Nor did she take much note of footsteps approaching or the faint protest of the hinges as the morning-room door swung open. She assumed it was Aubery, perhaps coming to coax her into riding out with him and Lianna before luncheon. In spite of her preoccupation with her own difficulties, she was beginning to notice a degree of attentiveness in Aubery toward Lianna that his behavior in leveling Francis in Lianna's defense the other day seemed to underscore.

Philippa decided that the lines she had just written were no more expressive of the feelings she wished to convey than any of her other attempts, and she crumpled the paper before turning in her chair to greet her brother. But the man she beheld was not Aubery, but Crispin.

He said not a word but withdrew from an inner pocket two pieces of folded paper, one of which he held out to her. Philippa read it through. It was a legal document of several pages, and after reading the first few paragraphs, she became aware that it was a marriage settlement. She skipped over much of the convoluted legal language, which she did not entirely understand in any case, but the gist of it soon became clear. The settlement so tied up her inheritance that her control of it was absolute. Crispin relinquished all claim to her fortune and any right to dispose of it; she might even leave it where she would in the event of her own demise. In addition, there was a provision for her jointure that was generous in the extreme and quite unconditional.

Philippa read until about the middle of the third page and then she put the document down on the desk and looked up at Crispin, who had stood watching her while she read the settlement papers. Still silent, he held out the second folded paper, a single sheet this time.

When Philippa opened it, she knew at once what it was: a special license for them to be married. Her eyes filled with unexpected tears and she dropped the license to her lap, covering her face with her hands.

Crispin dropped to one knee beside her and put his arms around her. "This was not supposed to make you cry," he said gently into her ear.

"I—I don't know what to say to you, Cris. I am so ashamed for doubting you."

"Say that you are hopelessly, violently in love with me and that you don't doubt you shall expire with impatience until we use this to be married at last."

Philippa laughed through her tears and repeated as word-perfect as she could what he had just said. He got to his feet and brought her up with him, embracing her and kissing her with fervor.

How much longer this behavior, so lost to all propriety, would have gone on, or where it would have led, could not be known, for the family had returned from church while Philippa was reading the settlements, and Aubery chose that moment to seek his sister out, actually having the intention of asking her to ride out on the estate with him and Lianna. Startled by the interruption, Philippa and Crispin parted but without the usual embarrassment of couples found making love to each other in the middle of the morning.

Aubery was frowning, but more with confusion than disapproval. "Do you mean you *are* to marry Cris after all?" he asked his sister, incredulous. "Damme, you ain't fickle, girl, you're demented."

"Thank you, Aubery," Crispin said dryly. "I

thought you said the other day that you would not object to having me for a brother."

"I shall not mind it in the least. I only hope you know what you're about. Pip's forever accusing me of inconstancy, but if I were you, I'd keep her locked up in some remote corner of the house. She'll be plighting her troth with the chimney sweep next."

"Is Philippa coming with us?" Lianna asked, coming into the room. "Should I change into my habit or . . ." She broke off as she saw Crispin. He had one hand lightly resting on Philippa's waist, and although Philippa's eyes were a trifle swollen, she did not look unhappy—very much the reverse. "Oh, Pip, I am so happy for you," she said, sizing up the situation at once.

Philippa and Crispin exchanged smiles. "I have convinced your cousin that I am the best the Glennon family has to offer," he said to Lianna, "and she would be foolish beyond permission to pass me up. Now, Philippa will be more than your cousin, she will be your sister."

At first this seemed to please Lianna very much, but then her pretty face clouded over and she blurted, "Will that make Aubery my brother? Oh, dear, shall we need special dispensation, then?" she asked Aubery.

"Special dispensation for what?" Philippa asked warily.

Lianna colored prettily and Aubery drew her next to him. "I know I shouldn't have spoken to Lia until I have written to Uncle Henry, but he has not so mean a nature as Cousin Dominic and I am confident he will approve. I have already spoken to Aunt Charlotte, and she has said that if Uncle Henry agrees, she will have no objection, provided that we wait for the wedding until after I achieve my majority in December." He looked down at Lianna as he spoke while she looked adoringly up at him. "It will be torture to wait, but I am not blind to Aunt Charlotte's objections. I fancied myself in love with Lydia Wright when it was nothing more than infatuation. Inconstancy does seem to be a family trait," he added with a grin for his sister. "I shan't change my mind or my heart this time, though."

"Do you think he will change his mind this time?" Crispin asked his beloved as they sat on a sofa in the morning room after Aubery and Lianna had left to inform Lady Carnavon that there was to be yet another wedding in the family.

Philippa smiled at him lovingly and shook her head. "I think that constancy is finally in season for the Worths."

About the Author

Originally from Pennsylvania, Elizabeth Hewitt lives in New Jersey. She enjoys reading and history, and is a fervent Anglophile. Music is also an important part of her life; she studies voice and sings with her church choir and with the New Jersey Choral Society.

⊘ SIGNET HISTORICAL GOTHIC

Her lips were still warm from the imprint of his kiss, but now Silvia knew there was nothing to protect her from the terror of Serpent Tree Hall. Not even love. Especially not love. . . .

DARK SPLENDOR

ANDREA PARNELL

Lovely young Silvia Bradstreet had come from London to Colonial America to be a bondservant on an isolated island estate off the Georgia coast. But a far different fate awaited her at the castle-like manor: a man whose lips moved like a hot flame over her flesh . . . whose relentless passion and incredible strength aroused feelings she could not control. And as a whirlpool of intrigue and violence sucked her into the depths of evil . . . flames of desire melted all her power to resist. . . .

Coming in September from Signet!